I0549240

Sweet Music
on
Moonlight Ridge

a novel

Ramey Channell

St. Leonard's Field

Alabama   Georgia

Author's Note

This book is a work of fiction. Names, characters, places, and incidents are used fictitiously, and any resemblance to actual persons, living or dead, and actual events is purely coincidental.

All rights reserved. No part of this book may be used or reproduced by any means, graphic, electronic, or mechanical, including photocopying, recording, taping, or by any information storage retrieval system without the written permission of the publisher except in the case of brief quotations embodied in articles and reviews.

Reviewers may quote passages for use in periodicals, newspapers, or broadcasts provided credit is given to *Sweet Music on Moonlight Ridge* by Ramey Channell and St. Leonard's Field.

Citations:
p. 28 – The Frog – anonymous
p.45 – variation of Has Everybody Heard About Harry – anonymous
p. 46 – The Peanut Song – anonymous
p.60 – Green Pastures – traditional hymn, anonymous
p.66 – Brylcreem jingle used by permission, Combe Inc. White Plains, NY
p.83-84 – Desdemona's Song, also known as Willow, Willow by William Shakespeare (1564-1616) , from *The Tragedy of Othello, the Moor of Venice*, Act IV scene 3

Copyright © 2015 Ramey Channell
All rights reserved.
ISBN 13: 978-0991187706
ISBN-10: 0991187709

First published in 2010 by Chalet Publishers LLC

"A person first reading *Sweet Music* encounters the soft and authentic Southern voice of a narrator who recounts a family tale so outrageous and surrealistic that it must undoubtedly be true. From 'doodle bugs,' to mythic monsters, to the great authentic recipes at the end, this narrative is a wonderful odyssey for the ear and imagination alike."
— Dale Short, author, *The Shining, Shining Path*

"If you didn't grow up on Moonlight Ridge, you will wish you had. Tom Sawyer and Huckleberry Finn would be right at home. I promise you laughter, adventure, and the sweet music of a place and time you will not soon forget."
— Teresa Thorne, author, *Noah's Wife*

"The antics of the delightfully eccentric Greenberry family had me laughing from the first page, and by the time I'd reluctantly finished their story, I wanted to pack up and move to Eden, Alabama. I can't wait to share this charming and original book with friends and family!"
— Cassandra King, author, *The Same Sweet Girls*

"A story as delightful as a walk in the rain, full of wonder and freshness."
— Irene Latham, author, *Leaving Gee's Bend*

This book is dedicated to my cousin, Donnie Lee Nock, and in memory of my father's cousin, Henry Whitner.

Acknowledgements

Thanks to the following people who read early drafts of this story and gave encouragement: Joanne Cage, Susan Cleveland, India Dyer, Sally Freind, Mable Hecht, Buffy Hosey, Jackie Matte, Nina Miller and Brad Watson. Special thanks to Cassandra King, Irene Latham, Dale Short and Teresa Thorne.

Special thanks to my sisters, Joanne Cage and Susan Cleveland for their talented assistance in constructing a fine red Drunkard's Path quilt, just like Lily Claire's.

Thanks to Jed Cage for his technological help and expertise.

Thanks to Roy Burkett for the sweet music.

Most of all, thanks to my parents, grandparents and all my family, for all the magical stories.

Introduction

Lily Claire is not my name, but I used to be a lot like her. I once lived on a mountain like Moonlight Ridge, and it seemed like a mystical place then. Looking back, I still think there was more than a little bit of enchantment there.

My cousin and I lived and played like wild children of the woods and we never imagined that there was any life or any home more desirable than our own.

Back then, we accepted the magic of the mountain with very few questions, and we didn't think there was anything unbelievable about it. Every experience, every event, and every aspect of the mountain itself may have been beyond the realm of the ordinary, but to those of us who called it home, it was just life 'out on the mountain'.

It was often a dangerous place, threatened with thunderstorms, rattlesnakes, thorns and briars, poison oak and poison ivy, stinging insects, dangerous heights, and stealthy beasts of the night. But the good things always outweighed the bad. There were arrowheads to be found in the plowed fields, astounding fossils to be picked up beside dusty trails, blackberries and wild plums, wild grapes and muscadines in the trees, little round rocks that had sand or crystals inside when you cracked them open, and animals who were, if not tame, at least tolerant.

On clear nights when there was no moon, the sky was so crowded with stars that it looked like a big bowl of diamonds turned upside down. And when the moon was full, the landscape on the mountain was transformed into an eerily beautiful scene filled with mesmerizing light.

We knew exactly what the birds were saying when they called to each other — at least, we thought we understood them. And we understood the hearts of the people who made up our family and our community.

I hope you will enjoy discovering these fascinating people, the fantastic creatures, and the enchanted legacy that is *Sweet Music on Moonlight Ridge*. For me, it has been a wonderful journey back to a magical place.

– Ramey Channell

One

My Blood Kin

My cousin was named after our great-grandfather, William Theophilus Greenberry, who had been dead a long, long time when my cousin and I were born, and who had been a crazy man when he was alive.

I don't know why, but it seems like our part of the country just breeds crazy people. We're from Moonlight Ridge, out on the mountain near a little town called Eden, Alabama. When you leave Eden, you go straight up the mountain, and that's where the Greenberrys have always lived.

My Great-granddaddy W.T. Greenberry was a naturalist, and he was absolutely enthralled with bugs. He kept every single dad-blamed old bug that he ever found, dead ones and live ones, all over his house. My Granny Rilla, W.T.'s only child, whose full name was Ianthe Marilla, told me how he always had jars and cages full of all manner of bugs, some so horrible to look at, they made her afraid to go to sleep at night when she was little because Great-granddaddy was always forgetting to close cages and put lids on the jars.

But sooner or later, every one of the old bugs

would die, and then W.T. would stick them on a board with a straight pin and attempt to take their picture. He had one of those old-fashioned cameras with the black cloth you had to stick your head under and the tray full of exploding powder. Granny said he blew up a lot of his dead bugs.

But some of his dead bug photographs turned out. I even have a few of them hanging on my bedroom wall: black and white photos with edges ragged and brown and the scientific names, real or made-up, scrawled across the bottom of the picture in Great-granddaddy's wild loopy handwriting. There's a big black beetle with white circles around its eyes, *Alaus oculatus elateridae;* a doodle bug, *Hesperoleon abdominalis;* and a roach, *Orthoptera periplaneta*. It's a really big roach. Granny said that W.T. told her it came from Cuba on a ship during the Spanish American War. The poor thing! Trying to get away from the war, it came all the way to Alabama on a ship and ended up being caught by a crazy man. It just goes to show you.

But it wasn't just bugs that Great-granddaddy W.T. Greenberry was interested in. He went on excursions, Granny said, into the woods all over Moonlight Ridge and all around Alabama, and wrote about leaves and weeds and flowers that he saw. He'd bring home specimens and try to get them to grow in his yard, and make up names for the ones he didn't know the names of. Granny said he perfectly loved a trillium! But Granny also said he mostly went on those excursions just to get away from the house, and that he always took a bottle of whiskey with him, and he always came home when the bottle was empty.

And Great-granddaddy W.T. Greenberry purely doted on possums. Every time Granny told me this, she'd always shake her head and say how her mother, my great-grandmother, hated, abhorred, and despised possums, with their little beady eyes and their long old tails scraping around through the house. W.T. brought so many possums into the house that my great-grandmother, Augusta Greenberry, would open the back door and call Rich Man and Poor Man, the hunting dogs, into the house to chase the possums out, and they'd raise a ruckus all through the house, chasing possums up the draperies and under tables and up the bed posts. And Great-granddaddy W.T.? He'd grab anything he could find, a broom or a rifle or an umbrella, and go chasing the dogs and leaping over chairs and devonettes and yelling.

"Run, possums, run! Run, little possums!" W.T. implored the scattering possums as he tore through the house in a state of mad panic.

"Ye bastards! Ye cursed bastards! Great sons of bitches!" he bawled at the hounds, warping at the big old clumsy dogs, whacking them across their heads until they ran back out the door, whining and yelping.

Then W.T. would yell out the back door, "Hounds from Hell! Murderous mongrels! Keep away from my marsupials!"

Granny said you could hear him all the way to Eden.

He'd sit in his big old chair in front of the fireplace, cuddling and petting one of the grimacing possums, looking in its ears and inspecting its tail for possible injuries. That's when he'd accuse Great-grandmother Augusta of not having any natural human affection for the poor possums, and he'd tell her it was precisely that sort of scurrilous attitude that hastened the demise of the dodo bird and the great auk.

15

"*Americanus marsupialus!*" he'd holler at her, shaking a possum at her with its old tail a'swayin' in the breeze. "Could be on the precipice of extinction! The very precipice!"

Then he'd start in singing, as loud as he could bellow, the church song "Dona Nobis Pacem." Except in his version the words were "Oh, don't I know this possum?"

Granny said this kind of an uproar happened as regular as clockwork, from the time she was a little girl until she was grown up, and that some of her friends were afraid to come inside the house because of the bugs and possums and dogs and the cussin' and chasin'. Then after she grew up, she married my granddaddy, a part-Cajun from South Alabama named Jack Levert, and settled down to a normal life.

The way the story goes, the Leverts moved up here to Moonlight Ridge when Paw Paw Jack was nothing but a spindly-legged little boy, white skinned with a head full of curly black hair. Granny says her daddy made fun of them, a wagonload of Cajuns carrying nothing with them but a pirogue and a fiddle and a couple of sacks full of pecans. Great-granddaddy W.T. told them they'd have no use for a pee-row up here in the hills of Alabama, so old Pere Levert turned the wooden boat upside-down and used it for the roof of a little portico on the east side of the rambling wood-frame house he built. Forever after that, the little porch was known as the pee-row portico.

That's where Granny said she first met Jack Levert when they were kids. He was playing his daddy's fiddle out on the pee-row portico, some sort of eerie haunting melody. It was an Irish tune called "Believe Me if All Those Endearing Young Charms,"

16

with words written by a famous man named Thomas Moore in about 1800. But, being a Cajun and all, Jack sang the words to "Au Clair de la Lune" instead. Granny said it was the most beautiful, melancholy sound she'd ever heard, and she knew right then that he was the boy she wanted to marry when they grew up.

To the best of my knowledge, Paw Paw Jack Levert never cared one way or the other about Great-granddaddy W.T.'s marsupials, which Jack called "all dem pie-sumes." He certainly never was afraid to come calling at the Greenberry house full of dogs and bugs and possums and pots full of strange stinky plants all over the place.

"All dem pie-sumes," he'd drawl. "Dey make the plass more happy. I tell you dat for sure!"

By the time he was a teen-ager he was playing poker for a living and making homemade fiddles on the side. Great-granddaddy W.T. never objected to his daughter marrying Jack Levert because he loved to hear Jack play the fiddle, and he said the music calmed his possums down when they got fidgety, and that it helped his plant specimens to take root. He claimed the only reason that God ever made a Cajun was because He must have loved beautiful fiddle music. Granny said that sometimes when Jack was playing his fiddle, especially when he played his version of "Au Clair de la Lune," Great-granddaddy W.T. would pick up a pair of fat possums, one under each arm, and dance around the house swaying to the music and humming along.

So anyway, it surely seems to me like my Aunt Rachel would have known better than to name my cousin after Great-granddaddy William Theophilus Greenberry. Couldn't she have guessed that it was purely asking for trouble, to name a sweet little baby boy after a total lunatic with an unnatural affection for bugs and possums?

But that's what she did.

William Theophilus Greenberry Nock.

I just called him Willie T.

Two

Coming Into This World

Willie T. and I were born on the same day, in the same hospital, and would have been delivered by the same doctor, but Dr. Carlisle called in help when he saw how things were going.

My mother, Sara Onselle Nash, and her sister, my aunt Rachel Bodicea Nock, were in the same hospital room when they went in to have me and Willie T. The way the story goes, my daddy, Sam Nash, and Willie T.'s daddy, Buddy Nock, had been out drinking all night the night before, and so they spent most of that day we were born sleeping on the gray leather benches in the hospital waiting room. So, it was mostly Granny and Dr. Carlisle that tried to handle things when my mama and her sister both went crazy at the same time and started throwing bedpans and lamps and water pitchers.

And cryin' and cussin'! Granny said that if it hadn't been for her upbringing with the bugs and the possums and Rich Man and Poor Man, that she never would have lived through the day me and Willie T. were born. I guess it just goes to show you.

By the time pitiful old Dr. Driggers, drunk as a lord, came stumbling into the Eden Hospital to help out Dr. Carlisle, the floor of the hospital room was covered with broken glass and spilled water and all the pitchers and bedpans and medical supplies, and my mama and Aunt Rachel had each other by the throat trying to strangle each other to death. The gray metal table that had been between the two hospital beds had been thrown through the window, shattering glass and landing in an arby-vida bush. With no obstacle between the two hospital beds, Mama and Aunt Rachel were able to get ahold of each other, ripping hospital gowns, pulling out each other's hair, and giving each other black eyes and busted lips. I don't guess anybody really knows why they lit into each other like that. Mama and Aunt Rachel both claimed it was a reaction to some drug they were given, and they swore that neither one of them would ever trust a doctor again. Granny says they both had always been a little high-strung.

So, when it finally came time for me and Willie T. to be born, Dr. Driggers did the best he could with Aunt Rachel, and Dr. Carlisle told my mother she had absolutely no normal maternal instincts.

They say that Willie T. and I were born at the very same time, that we both started crying at the very same moment, and that we looked so much alike we could have been twins.

As soon as they saw us, Aunt Rachel and Mama started crying again, because Aunt Rachel wanted a girl and Mama wanted a boy. But after a while, they both settled down and even smiled a little when Granny said we looked for the world like two baby possums.

Dr. Carlisle, who had one green eye and one brown eye, cried too, after wrestling all day with Mama and dodging flying objects. He threatened to give up the medical practice altogether, but then he went to laughing and said, "Well, I'll tell you what, this beats all I've ever seen! Don't this beat all? I've got to get a picture of this!"

He was so tickled by the whole affair that he called his wife on the telephone and told her to grab her Kodak camera and hurry to the Eden Hospital and take Mama and Aunt Rachel's picture. The photograph, which is still hanging on the wall of Dr. Carlisle's old office to this day, shows the two beat-up women sitting up in the hospital beds, side-by-side, holding me and Willie T. and smiling sheepishly with their swollen lips and black eyes.

My daddy brought Mama a bouquet of white lilies-of-the-valley that he'd picked out of Granny Rilla's garden, and that's when they decided to name me Lily Claire Carlisle Nash. Uncle Buddy brought Aunt Rachel a bunch of yellow stink-weeds that he'd pulled by the side of the road, and that's when she decided to name my cousin William Theophilus Greenberry Nock.

Three

The Games We Played

Willie T. and I pretty much grew up cheek-by-jowl. Aunt Rachel and Uncle Buddy Nock lived in a little white house on top of a hill, about a half-a-mile away from me and Mama and Daddy. When I was little, it seemed like a long, long way, but by the time Willie T. could walk good, and if the weather was fair, he started showing up at our house almost every morning after our daddies had gone to work. Aunt Rachel would get busy doing something and take her eyes off of him for one split second, and he'd sneak off quicker than you could say Jack Robinson. It wasn't long until Aunt Rachel saw that it was a hopeless case. So, if it was raining or too cold outside, she just gave in and brought him to us in her car. She said he cried and pitched such a conniption-fit to come to our house that she had to let him come or he'd break out with the nettle rash and drive her crazy, and she couldn't polish her fingernails or read a magazine or work a cross-word puzzle because of him.

I got in the habit of watching for him from Mama's bedroom window where I could see down the road, and as soon as I saw him trotting toward the house, or saw Aunt Rachel's car slowly approaching on the gravelly unpaved road, I lit out running through the house in a fit of irrational glee, squealing, "Here comes Willie T! Here comes Willie T!" to the tune of "Here Comes Santy Claus." I got so accustomed to him being there all the time, for better or for worse, and our whole house, and the whole woods, and the whole world, for that matter, seemed boring and empty when he wasn't around.

But he was the meanest little booger you'd ever want to see. In the early years, before we started to school, we fought just about as much as we played. And then it got so that, for the most part, we couldn't tell the difference between playing and fighting. Granny told Mama and Aunt Rachel that they had marked us by fighting like they did at the hospital when we were being born, and there was nothing to be done about it now.

I remember Granny's patient voice repeating the same thing every time Mama or Aunt Rachel complained or worried about me and Willie T. fighting so much.

"You've marked those two children, it's as sure as the world, with all that rigamarole at the hospital, and now you've got it to live with. It sure goes to show you; your chickens will always come home to roost."

I believe what she meant was that Willie T. and I were as good as ruined, and now Mama and Aunt Rachel had to keep us, come hell or high water, and it was just catch as catch can from here on out.

We really never had a lot of store-bought toys when we were real little, some cap-guns from the ten-cent-store, and plenty of marbles and maybe a doll or two.

23

The dolls were all cut open and sewed up again with big black stitches, over and over again. We sewed all kinds of things up inside them: marbles, rocks, empty aspirin tins, hairpins, crayons. Granny showed us how to sew the stitches with her great big old needles that she used because she couldn't see how to thread the little ones, and Mama didn't care as long as we didn't sew up something that she needed, like a thimble or a box of matches. Or her lipstick.

By the time we were in the first grade, we could make practically anything we wanted to keep ourselves entertained. We made bows and arrows; shot them at each other even though we were assured by our mothers that we would put somebody's eye out. We made kites with long tails of all-different-colored calico rags, and sometimes we were able to go off by ourselves to fly them; but most of the time my daddy got ahold of them and left me and Willie T. like Ol' Dan Tucker, just standin' there lookin'. Daddy could get a kite so high it looked like a tiny dot, way, way up in the blue sky.

If the weather wasn't too cold outside, we went out under the shed where Daddy kept firewood to look for doodle bugs. You can always spot a doodle bug hole because they are round and shaped like a shallow funnel with a little deep hole in the middle. Willie T. and I were expert doodle bug catchers. Sticking a tiny little twig down into the hole, we stirred around and around chanting, "Doodle bug, doodle bug, come out of your hole. Doodle bug, doodle bug, come out of your hole. Come get your milk 'n bread, milk 'n bread, milk 'n bread."

But once you catch a doodle bug, there's not much to do except look at it, and say "Yep, that's a doodle bug," then put him back in his hole. They scurry down the sandy sides of the funnel and back into the tiny round opening as fast as their little doodle bug legs can go. And ugly? *Hesperoleon abdominalis* is a gruesome sight.

Whenever we got bored and started complaining about having nothing to play with, Granny Rilla told us to gather up pinecones and make like they were possums and send them to school. The two of us spent many long hot summer days teaching rows of pinecones, perfectly lined up in their invisible desks, the ABCs and 123s. Pinecones have sharp little barbs on the end of each of their 'petals', and our fingers stayed scratched and sore all the time. Willie T. complained constantly.

"Them possums is mean!" he'd gripe, wiping a bloody finger on the front of his shirt. But he talked to them in a sweet high pitched voice, just like a mama talking to her little baby.

About the time we were in the first grade, Willie T. came up with two new games. One was climbing trees and jumping down on top of me when I was least expecting it. He could jump down from a limb so high, you'd think it would kill him. But it never did. I believe he was born with springy legs.

The other game was his own perplexing brand of hiding-seek. After he counted to a hundred faster than a flea on a greased hound-dog, and I got hid from him with my heart just a-pounding, he'd yell out, in the most irritating voice you could imagine, "My nose eetches, I smell peaches, yonder comes a woman with a hole in her breeches." If that didn't cause me to hop up from my hiding place to bless him out for talking any such a way, he'd start calling out in a scary creepy

25

voice, "Stranger knows your na-ame. Stranger knows your na-ame," as he crept around looking for me. It's hard to say why, but that always made me feel like a possum had run over my grave, and Willie T. knew it.

Whenever he found me, we'd both tear out screaming and running, slapping and swatting at each other, squealing in terror, afraid of getting knocked down or ending up with black eyes, as we sometimes did. During one of these episodes, I accidentally knocked out one of his front teeth that had been so loose for days that it was just barely hanging in his mouth.

"My TOOTH!" he screamed, tears streaming down his sweaty dirty face, then he doubled up his fist and whopped me square in the mouth sending my front tooth, which had not been loose at all, flying through the air. Then the two of us went scrambling home, wailing, holding our respective teeth in our grimy hands, each swearing that the other was "sure in trouble now!"

Willie T. ran off toward his house and for once I was glad to see him going in that direction. I ran home and raced in the front door, yelling "Mama! Mama!" as loud as I could possibly holler.

Daddy was sitting in the living room listening to the radio and Mama was in the kitchen. I flew through the front door, letting the screen door slam. Daddy jumped straight up when he saw me, and Mama rushed out of the kitchen. They both grabbed hold of me and started turning me first one way then another, trying to see what was wrong with me I guess. I wiped my hand across my mouth and there was a smear of blood.

"Why, what happened to *you*?" Mama asked, her face right up close to mine.

"What's the matter, baby?" Daddy asked.

"Willie T. knocked my tooth out! Knocked me a sky-winding! Look!"

I held out my hand and displayed the estranged tooth that had so recently been part of me but was now a separate thing. "Look!" I repeated.

Whenever my daddy hears a big noise that scares him, he always jumps up and says, "There!" like he's locating where the noise came from. When something just totally amazes him till he doesn't know what to say, he says "They!" I truly believe he is the only person in the whole wide world who expresses himself that way.

He bent over, looking at the tooth in my hand like he'd never seen a tooth in his life before, and said "They!"

"What in the world made Willie T. do such a thing?" Mama asked, her voice high-pitched and shaky like she was about to cry. Daddy nudged my mouth open and peered into it like he was lookin' at the most interesting thing he had ever seen in the whole world.

"They," he repeated slowly. "Came out clean as a whistle, didn't it?" He sounded kinda proud, like he was appraising some kind of wonderful accomplishment.

"Sam!" Mama scolded, and Daddy looked up at her from his crouched position, all sulled up like she had accused him of something.

"Why did Willie T. hit you hard enough to knock your tooth out?" Mama asked again.

"Well, it was just because I had already hit him and knocked *his* old tooth out," I explained. "But it was that

27

old loose one that's been a' danglin' all this long time, for days and days."

Daddy made a loud spluttering sound, then busted out laughing.

"Well, I'll say!" he exclaimed. "Look at that, Sara. Knocked it plumb out of her mouth!" And he clapped his hands one loud smack, then laughed again.

"Well, it's not funny," Mama stated, wiping my face with the tail of her apron. Then she went in the kitchen and fixed me some warm salt-water to rinse out my mouth.

That night I got ten cents under my pillow from the tooth fairy and eventually our teeth grew back in, and the new ones had stronger roots, so it all turned out okay. After that, whenever we lost other baby teeth, Willie T. always acted like a big-shot and bragged, "It ain't nothin' to it, losin' milk teeth." That like to irked me to death, but I never did remind him how he'd acted like a big old baby about his stupid old tooth that I knocked out.

There was one thing that always seemed to come natural to both of us, and that was music. Dancing and singing was as natural to us as breathing. We woke up every morning and went to sleep every night singing Paw Paw Jack's sad sounding "Au Clair de la Lune," even though neither one of us knew exactly what the words were about.

"I believe it's about some poor old feller in the jail house," Daddy told us. "And he's tryin' to write a letter to his sweetheart, by the light of the moon. That's what 'Oh, clair day la loon' means. And then he hollers, 'Open up the door, for the Lord's sake!' "

We all wondered how such a sad sounding song could be so funny.

When it came to dancing, we learned a different kind of dance from every person we knew, and made up some of our own. Granny taught us how to square dance and do-si-do. Mama taught us the minuet, Aunt Rachel taught us the polka, and Daddy taught us how to do the jitterbug. We put it all together in our own wild rambunctious dance, along with the stiff-starch, and sometimes right in the middle of a game of marbles or hop-scotch or a fight, we'd both break into a spontaneous fit of dancing. Whenever Uncle Buddy Nock caught us dancing, he laughed at us and told us we were just "cuttin' the fool." He said the be-bop was the only dance that was worth anything, but my daddy made him reconsider in favor of the jitterbug.

About the time we started the second grade, Aunt Rachel and Uncle Buddy Nock got a television set and Willie T. discovered Gene Krupa, the drummer, and he decided we needed to learn how to play the drums. We got an old metal washtub and a tin water bucket and some tin lard cans and carried them out into the woods behind my house, and we'd stand out there beating and banging out rhythms while we sang songs we'd heard on the radio. We used dead sticks called Tommy-knockers, the long kind with a big round knot on the end, for our drumsticks, and we managed to make a lot of noise. When Daddy went out hunting he said he couldn't shoot a single squirrel anywhere near our house because Willie T. and I made so much noise out in the woods, we had run them all off. He said there wasn't a squirrel for miles around.

Possums were another question altogether. You can't hardly scare a possum with noise or music or banging on a drum. They'll just sull up somewhere and wait it out.

Then, wouldn't you know it, Willie T. fell in love with baseball and he got on the Eden Pee Wee Baseball Bandits Team. He got the big-head over being a Baseball Bandits celebrity and gave up the drumming, and we were immediately overcome by squirrels.

Another one of our favorite activities was playing in the rain. In the hot summertime you could smell a rain coming before it ever got to you, and the smell always made my mouth water. If Mama said there wasn't gonna be any thunder and lightning, we'd run around in the front yard until we were soaking wet, singing, "Rain, rain, go away. Come again another day."

Once in the very hottest part of the summer, Willie T. and I were playing in the rain when all of a sudden a multitude of little tiny frogs started falling from the sky.

"Why, look," I said when I saw the first one. "There's a little baby frog."

Immediately another one plopped down beside me. Then another and another.

"Lookee there!" Willie T. squealed. "There's one! There's one!"

Tiny frogs were falling everywhere, and when they hit the ground, they began hopping and leaping around us in the rain. One or two of them hopped against my legs, and they felt soft and cool and wet on my skin, just like the raindrops.

"Mama! Mama!" I called. "Come see all the little froggies!"

Willie T. broke into a shrill chorus of "Froggy Went a' Courtin" as Mama appeared on the front porch. She watched for a while, and then came out into the drizzly yard where she recited a poem as she leaned over to inspect the tiny amphibians.

> What a remarkable bird the frog are.
> When him sit, him almost lie.
> When him hop, him almost fly.
> He got no tail at all, most hardly.

The poem made Willie T. and me giggle with delight, and we started hopping around, imitating the little frogs.

"Well, y'all come on in, now," she told us. "You're fixing to step on the poor little things and squash them, there's so many of them. Come on, now."

The three of us tiptoed across the yard and up onto the front porch. We turned and watched as the rain began to slack off a little, and the sun broke through the clouds.

"Y'all come on in and get dried off. I'll make us some popcorn," Mama said.

Of course, Willie T. got a popcorn hull stuck in his throat, and pitched a fit.

In just a little bit, we looked outside and the bright sun was sparkling in the fast-drying mud puddles, and most of the tiny frogs had hopped away. When Daddy came home from work, we tried to find some to show him, but we only found one little bitty one, sitting under the front porch steps, all alone.

"Well now, frogs do good work," Daddy told me and Willie T. "They catch bugs and flies and skeeters. We'd be eat up without them. We been needin' some more frogs."

Then, wouldn't you know it, he started in singing "Froggy Went a' Courtin", and Willie T. just beamed.

It made me feel good to know that right when we

were needing frogs, God just up and threw a bunch of them down here to us. I guess it just goes to show you.

The only time we ever got in trouble over the rain was one time when we were in the third grade and me and Willie T. made it start raining on a clear sunny day.

It was Spring Break and we were out of school for a whole week, and I reckon we were getting a little bored. Somehow or another we both got to talking about doing a rain dance. Mama had been in the kitchen all morning, defrosting the Frigidaire, and Daddy was at work, laying bricks for a new bank in downtown Birmingham, and the sky was as blue as a bird's egg, not a cloud anywhere. Willie T. and I were sitting on the living room floor, coloring in a color book till we were perfectly tired of staying in the lines.

It was a color book about Indians, and I had colored Indians in canoes and Indians standing outside their teepees and Indians gazing up at the stars. Then I came to a picture of an Indian man dancing, and at the bottom of the page, it said "Doing the Rain Dance." I stopped coloring and looked at that picture for a minute.

"Hey, Willie T., you wanta do a rain dance?" I asked.

"Huh? Do a what?" he asked, without looking up from his Indian on a horse.

"A rain dance," I repeated, pushing his hand away from the page.

"Rain dance? You wanta do one?" Willie T. asked back. He turned the color book around and looked at the picture of the dancing man for a second.

"Let's go do it! I'm dang tired of colorin'," he announced, hopping up from the floor.

"Mama, we're goin' outside to do a rain dance," I called. Mama was busy in the kitchen, and I don't think she was really paying us any attention.

"Okay," was all she said, so we quickly scampered out the door into the beautiful sunny front yard.

Now, I can't recall anybody ever teaching me and Willie T. how to do a rain dance. It was just like every other kind of dancing, I guess; we just knew what to do and how to do it. But we certainly didn't expect it to work so fast!

We started dancing around in a circle, stepping slowly down on one foot, then sort of hopping onto the other foot. We both began chanting, and not paying much attention to the sky, just dancing and hopping, dancing and hopping. Suddenly, a strong cool breeze blew across the yard, and my cotton sundress whipped around in the wind, and rain started pouring out of the sky so fast we didn't know what to do next. Both of us were soaked through and through before we could get onto the front porch, and Mama hurried out the front door with a sort of wild look on her face.

"What did y'all do?" she wailed, gazing out at the downpour like she'd never seen a drop of precipitation in her lifetime.

Willie T. was wiping rain off his face and shaking his head to get all the rainwater out of his bristly head of hair. "Rain dance," he answered, matter-of-factly.

"I never in my life!" Mama exclaimed. "Y'all get in the house and behave!"

We all went inside, feeling a little like something was wrong but none of us was sure what or why. At the door, Mama glanced back over her shoulder like she was afraid something awful might be coming after us.

After a little while the rain stopped, and Willie T. and I had dried off, and Mama was lurking out of sight in the kitchen. We had gone back to coloring, whispering to each other every now and then about how magic sure was a tricky business, when Daddy drove up into the yard and we heard his truck door slam shut.

As soon as he got through the front door, I could see by the look on his face that he was put out.

"When did it start raining here?" he asked, a little louder than he usually spoke.

Mama appeared out of the kitchen, and Willie T. and I lowered our heads and colored passionately. Mama asked Daddy why he was home from work in the middle of the day.

"It started raining so hard, we had to quit for the day, and they wasn't a cloud in the sky! I'm telling you it was a downpour! One minute the sky was as clear as it could be, and before we knew it, it was comin' down like the Dickens! I'll swear, I hate to miss a day of work!"

Mama looked at us, coloring away as hard as we could, and I knew she was going to tell on us.

"Lily Claire and Willie T. did a rain dance," she announced curtly, then she stomped back into the kitchen, shaking her dish towel with a loud snap.

"They! A rain dance?" Daddy exclaimed, slapping his hat against his pants leg. "What in the world did they do *that* for?" Then he threw his hat down on the devonette and glared at us like we were a couple of strangers he'd never laid eyes on before.

"Well, you've rurned us at work," he grunted, and stomped out of the living room. "I just want you to know you've caused us to miss a good day of work!

34

Um-um-um!"

Willie T. and I were a little scared, but we pretty much took it in stride. It was something we talked about every once in a while, but we never felt inclined to do another rain dance after that.

By the time Spring Break was over, we returned to school feeling almost back to normal, and we had already agreed not to tell anybody else about the rain dance. Not even our crazy old teacher. Then, before you could say Jack Robinson, the weeks flew by and our third year of grammar school was coming to an end.

Four

The Map

There's always that nervous feeling at the end of a school year, on the last day when you get your report card and see if you passed or failed. Willie T. and I were both in Miss Althea Bibb Tweedy's room in the third grade, and I honestly have to say that I think we were lucky to have been in her room, since she was just about the best third grade teacher in the whole world, even if everybody in Eden said that she had lost all her marbles, no doubt about it. She taught us how to draw every kind of bird you could think of, and helped every one of us in her class make a bird book with all our beautiful bird drawings in it. Miss Tweedy could draw birds better than anybody I've ever seen. And that didn't surprise anybody, because she actually kind of looked like a bird herself. All the boys called her Bird Legs.

But her favorite subject of all, something she liked even better than talking about birds, was telling us stories about all manner of heroes. She was always talking and going on about "hero this" and "hero that." She told us all about Johnny Appleseed and George

Washington Carver and a man who survived naked in the woods with nothing but a pocket knife. Miss Tweedy taught us how to break an apple in half on your knee, and how to plant a peanut and watch the little vine grow up out of it, and how to get a splinter out of your finger with a pocket knife. I guess I thought Johnny Appleseed was about the most wonderful person in the world, for planting all those apple trees, and I was eternally grateful to George Washington Carver for inventing peanut butter. But I couldn't help but wonder where that naked man kept his pocket knife, with nary a pocket to put it in.

But her very favorite hero of all was Eddie Rickenbacker, a guy who fell out of his airplane during the war. When she got to talking about him, she'd stand at the window looking all dreamy-eyed, gazing up into the sky like she expected to see him come plummeting down into the school-yard just any minute. Miss Tweedy just loved to tell about how Eddie Rickenbacker's britches and leather jacket filled up with air, and he came drifting down just like a balloon, and he landed in some trees and it didn't even kill him or anything, even though he fell about a hundred miles out of the sky. And that was just in World War I. When World War II came along, Eddie Rickenbacker crashed his airplane into the ocean, and floated around for about forty days and forty nights before somebody came and picked him up. So now he's a hero. And his brother, not wanting to be outsmarted, made beautiful guitars, which Miss Tweedy said didn't really make him a hero or anything, but was still a good enough occupation.

Anyway, on that last day of school, Willie T. and I were both pretty worried about passing and failing. I felt sure that I'd most likely passed, since I made all A's and had perfect attendance. But Willie T. was another question altogether. He missed a lot of days in the fall and the spring because he had the allergies, and when he *was* there the teacher always cried a lot.

But for better or worse, we both passed the third grade and said good-bye to Eddie Rickenbacker and Miss Althea Bibb Tweedy, and summer vacation stretched out in front of us without an end in sight. It always seemed to me like every summer something special would happen to make that summer unforgettable.

And sure enough, no sooner had school ended and summer vacation started before we made an amazing discovery that would launch us into the most unforgettable summer of all.

The woods around our house on Moonlight Ridge had always seemed full of magical secrets and possibilities. There were old trails and paths that were as ancient as the mountain itself. Willie T. and I roamed and tromped around in the very same places that our Great-granddaddy W.T. had explored, way back before we were even born, and every summer we'd make new discoveries and claim new areas as our own territory.

That summer after the third grade, we set out on a special mission, inspired by a most unusual map that we had found in the most surprising place you could imagine. As soon as we took one good look at that map, we struck out into the woods, thrilled by the certainty that it was a magic map that would lead us to a hidden treasure.

We had been walking about half an hour, following an old logging road through the lower meadow, up the side of the hill, then across the high meadow and into the woods. It was the first week of June, still early in the summer, but the Alabama heat had settled in early.

When the road forked into two barely visible paths leading in opposite directions down the steep side of the mountain, I started to worry a little. I stood there, squinting in the bright afternoon sun, staring as far as I could see down the path to my left, then the one to my right. In a way, I thought it seemed like an easy choice. One trail or the other.

"Well, it could be down this way," I said slowly, like answering a question nobody had asked.

"Yeah!" my cousin barked. "But it *could* be down 'at other way, too. And I ain't never been this far away from home by myself before," he added thoughtfully. "Have you, Lily C.?"

I just didn't feel like admitting that I hadn't. Instead, I turned and looked back the way we had come. The rocky old roadbed looked as forlorn as I felt. It was easy to see that the unpaved logging road hadn't been traveled for many years. I pulled a piece of tall grass and stuck it in my mouth to chew on.

"Well, Willie T., we're not really by ourselves. We're together," I suggested. "Anyway, I think we're gonna have to go back and take another look at the treasure map."

"Gyaah! You know Estaleen Howard ain't gonna let us back in that baby's mouth again today!" he yelped.

"Well, she *would*, if you'd quit yelling and scaring the poor little thing to death! Come on, let's go back," I said impatiently, pushing him with both hands as he turned and walked ahead of me along the rocky path.

39

The red plaid cotton shirt he was wearing, homemade by Aunt Rachel, was wet with sweat.

"I wouldn't have yelled if it hadn't tried to bite my finger off! That baby's got sharp teeth! Just like a dang pinecone possum!"

"Why, Willie T. Nock! That baby hasn't got any teeth at all! It's too little to have any teeth," I yelled at him as we both stumbled over the big loose rocks. "Haven't you ever been bit by a baby cow or a baby horse? It can't hurt you."

"A horse has got teeth!" he hollered.

"Well, maybe a horse *has* got teeth. But that little baby doesn't have any teeth. Not yet," I insisted. "It's not nearly old enough."

"Well, if it ain't got no teeth now," Willie T. whined mournfully, "it won't never have any, 'cause Mama said it's gonna die purty soon."

"That's not true!" I yelled, slapping him on the back as hard as I could. I heard the breath fly out of him, I hit him so hard. "That's a terrible thing to say! The poor little thing. That baby's not gonna die."

"Uh-huh," Willie T. insisted, paying no attention at all to the whack I had given him. "Mama said if a baby gets a map on its tongue, it'll die for sure, and they ain't nothin' you can do about it. And she said for us to stay away from it and to leave them Howards alone."

I stopped walking and stood watching my know-it-all cousin scrambling through a patch of tall weeds, still talking as if I was right behind him.

"Mama said when me and you was born, her and Aunt Sara (he pronounced it Aint Serrer) had to watch all the time to make sure we didn't get no map on our tongues, 'cause that's the worst thing that can happen if your baby gets one. And she tried to tell poor ole'

Estaleen that it was sure enough a map on her baby's tongue, and Estaleen, bein' a Howard and all, didn't know no better, and didn't believe it, but...Dammit! These weeds is makin' me itch! Come on, Lily C., let's go!"

Willie T. glanced back at me over his shoulder.

"I knew you'd done stopped way back there," he announced. "Come on, I wanta go home. I'm gettin' the nettle rash, and I'm hungry, and I bet we're in trouble for bein' gone so long."

I caught up with him and held onto the back of his shirt to help steady myself as we tediously picked our way up a rocky incline.

"I still don't believe that's true, anyway," I insisted. "That baby looks fatter and healthier than you do, and you're not dying. I believe that's just a tale. And quit telling Aunt Rachel everything, or we *will* get in trouble, and we'll never find the buried treasure if we don't get another look at that map."

Willie T. walked on silently for a minute. The dirt road had become level, and we both were out of breath from scrambling up the rocky hillside behind us.

"We're gonna have to draw a picture of that map," he announced. "You know it, Lily C.?" He reached back and swatted my hand away from the back of his shirt where I was still hanging on. "When we go back next time," he continued, "let's take a piece of paper and a pencil with us. You can draw so good, I bet you could copy it."

I thought about his suggestion all the rest of the way home, and I decided it sounded like such a good idea that I wished I had thought of it first. I guess it just goes to show you.

The very next morning, after eating scrambled eggs and grits and bacon so fast we almost choked, Willie T. and I hurried down the dusty road to the Howards' house. Willie T. carried a big biscuit in his hand, and continued eating as we ran along bare-footed over the sun-warmed red dirt.

"We've come to see your little baby again, Estaleen," I announced as politely as I could.

Estaleen Howard looked at us suspiciously through the screen door. The old wooden screen door was unpainted and the screen wire was rusty and sagging.

Estaleen was pale-skinned and scrawny and worried looking, but she laughed a lot and she loved to play jacks with me on her front porch. She beat me every time, but then she'd reach over and pat my hand and say, "You're gettin' better, Lily C. I'm gonna have to watch out or you'll beat me next time. Whoo-ee!"

Today she looked serious as she eyed Willie T. and me through the rusty screen.

"Well, I'll swear! You two are shore up to devilment," she whispered as she opened the screen door. The door scraped noisily across the wooden porch, and she touched it nervously as if to stop the noise.

"Y'all come on in, but be quiet," she whispered. "Cowboy's in the bed with one of them headaches he gits. He had to come home from the sawmill."

Willie T. and I looked at each other for just a second, then we nodded at each other without saying a word. It was the funniest thing; I don't know if we were nodding "Yes, we'll be quiet," or if we were nodding "Yes, Cowboy's always got a headache," or if we were nodding "Yes, we get to see the baby again."

But we followed behind Estaleen as silently as we could. We passed right by the bed where Cowboy Howard was lying, his face to the wall. As we tiptoed past the bed, he made a pitiful low moaning sound, to let us know that he was still alive and he knew we were there.

I held my breath till we got safely past him, because it seemed to me like Cowboy might jump up and grab us real quick, just to scare us. That was his favorite trick, when he didn't have a headache. More times than I could count, he'd sneak up on me and Estaleen when we were playing jacks on the front porch, and before we knew what had us, he'd jump up onto the porch, making a hideous roaring noise just like the wolfeener, the awfullest, scariest booger out on the mountain.

The noise the wolfeener made out in the woods was so scary, it would make your heart stop beating when you heard it.

"Eeee-eeee-oooo-whoooo-huh-huh-huh-huh," it would scream, with a greedy smacking noise at the end like it was just ready to eat you up. Most of the time you'd only hear it at night and most folks were cautious about walking around Moonlight Ridge after dark. But we had heard it a few times in the daytime, and once Daddy had seen it turn on his hunting dogs. He said it had a big head like a donkey and huge pointed teeth, and long shaggy hair like a big wolf.

Cowboy Howard's imitation of the wolfeener was so much like the real thing, he could fool us every time. It never failed, if we were bare-footed as usual, Estaleen and I would jump up yelling and trying to run, and we'd both step on those sharp pointy jacks with our bare feet, hopping and screaming and crying.

And Cowboy? He'd fall back against the nearest porch post with his hand over his heart, laughing and laughing! And then Estaleen would take a couple of weak swipes at him, wiping tears from her face and vowing, "I'll swun, you've about turned my liver over, this time!"

So, here we were, creeping around behind his back, while I held my breath. I felt sorry about his old headache, but still, I was a little afraid of him at the same time.

We made it safely past poor old sick Cowboy, and me and Willie T. and Estaleen crowded into the tiny room where the baby's bed was. Willie T. was holding onto my arm with both his hands, and he leaned over the side of the baby-bed to look at the little baby like he was looking at a dangerous animal.

"Well, hyar they is again!" Estaleen said in a hushed voice to her chubby little baby boy. The baby was lying there awake, and when he heard his mama's voice he started kicking both legs and waving his little fists in the air.

Willie T. giggled and leaned in a little closer to the smiling baby. "Why, look at it," he said, sounding surprised. "Lookee there, it's a'laughin' at me!"

We all started laughing, then Estaleen pointed toward the room where her husband was lying in bed and she said, "Shhh, y'all shush now." But the baby started kicking and waving his hands in the air again, and it was hard to keep from laughing at him.

"What's he doin'?" Willie T. asked. "He looks like he's tryin' to go somewheres."

"Well, maybe he is," Estaleen whispered, and she tickled the baby's fat little chin with her long thin finger. "I reckon he just wants to go off somewheres on

44

a big adventure. Whar you goin', Junior?" she whispered. "Whar you goin'?"

In reply, the baby squealed loudly and stuck his tongue out.

Willie T. and I almost jumped into the baby-bed on top of Junior.

"Look, look!" Willie T. yelped, leaning as close as he could to the baby's face. I glanced quickly at Estaleen and saw that she was staring at us like she thought we both had gone crazier than usual.

"Sh, shh!" she hissed. "Y'all quit that cuttin' up, now." From the other room, Cowboy let out a long pitiful moan.

My cousin and I looked at each other excitedly, and Willie T.'s eyes were so big and round he looked like Bu, the hoot-owl who lived in our woods. Then we both looked back at Baby Junior who decided to let out another ear-splitting squeal and stuck his little tongue out again.

Willie T.'s face was turning red and he started slapping me on the arm, then he grabbed for the pencil and paper I had stuffed in the pocket of my sundress. I tried to keep my crazy cousin from slapping me so hard, and the baby kept squealing, and Estaleen kept hissing, "Shh! Shh!" when suddenly, in the middle of this rambunctious free-for-all, Cowboy Howard himself appeared in the doorway between the two rooms, glaring at us and swaying back and forth like a pine tree in the wind. His face was deathly white, his eyes were bright red, and his thick bushy hair was standing straight up on top of his head.

"What in the worl' is a'goin' on in hyar?" he croaked. "Are y'all fightin' er what?"

Willie T. and I were still pushing one another, and Cowboy's sudden appearance startled Willie T. so bad that he grabbed ahold of me, pinching the daylights out of me.

"Ouch! Ouch!" I shrieked, trying to push my wild-eyed cousin away from me. Estaleen had a horrified look on her thin face as she frantically waved both her hands in the air, still shushing as hard as she could. Cowboy swayed forward and back with both his hands on top of his bushy head, like he was trying to keep it from exploding.

"Aa-aw! Aa-aw!" he moaned. "Y'all are tryin' to kill me, total. Aa-aw, my head!" He squinted his red eyes painfully and leaned his tall lanky frame over the foot of the baby-bed, staring at Junior who was still kicking and waving merrily. The baby squealed loudly again, and poor old Cowboy clapped his hands over his ears and threw himself backwards away from the baby-bed, a look of complete horror on his white face.

"I, God!" he wailed.

Estaleen jumped past me and Willie T. and grabbed ahold of her miserable husband. "Git on back in the bed, Honey," she crooned. "You best lay back down with yer head. Whoo-ee!"

As he was escorted to the bed, Cowboy cast a pitiful glance back at me and Willie T. and Baby Junior, who at that moment yawned a big wide yawn, giving all of us a good long look at that funny little tongue.

"Let's go, let's go!" I whispered anxiously.

I wanted to get away from there as fast as I could. For one thing, I felt so sorry for Cowboy with his horrible head, and I was a little bit scared by the way he looked with his red eyeballs and bushy hair. But mostly I wanted to get outside where I could get busy drawing what I had seen on Junior's tongue. It had a lot more curves and wiggles than I had remembered.

I pushed my flustered cousin away from the baby's bed, and we clattered out of the house and across the front porch, scattering a bunch of chickens who had gathered on the porch and were peering through the screen door, "pawk-pawk-pawking" inquisitively as we rushed out. The battered screen door slapped shut behind us with a loud bang. "Bye, Miss Estaleen. Thanks for lettin' us visit," I called as we made our hasty retreat. "Bye, Mr. Cowboy. I hope your awful head gets better."

Willie T. was chattering so fast that I couldn't understand a thing he was saying as we trotted up the dirt road, away from the Howard place. We stopped in a curve of the road and sat down in the shade of a persimmon tree. It was cooler under the small tree than it had been in Estaleen's little house. I looked up into the leafy branches above us and I could see tight little oddly shaped blossoms here and there amid the dark leaves. I knew that at the end of summer when school started back, there would be fat orange persimmons where those strange looking little flowers were now. I thought about the cinnamony-sweet persimmon cookies that our granny made for us every autumn after the first frost.

"I wish't you'd quit starin' around and wastin' time, Lily C.," my excited companion complained. "And start drawin' that map!" He helped me smooth out the wrinkled paper, and together we drew a picture of the map on Junior's tongue. We did such a good job, we were both surprised and happy when it was finished.

"You're a good map-drawer, Lily C.," Willie T.

47

exclaimed proudly. "I knew you could do it! Now, we'll just follow the map, and see what we find!"

"A treasure map! On a Howard baby's tongue! Who'd of thought it?"

Willie T. nodded enthusiastically. "Yep! I guess it just goes to show you!"

Five

Bad News

My mother and my father came from families as different as any two families could possibly be. Mama's family, the Greenberrys and Leverts, were all well-to-do landowners here in Moonlight Ridge, and according to my granny, were Quakers, French Huguenots, and Acadians who moved to this country from England and France way back in the 1600s seeking religious freedom. My daddy's family, the Nashes, originally spelled their name Naiche, and were mixed-bloods, part Apache. The Mescaleros and Chiricahuas came to Alabama in the 1800's when the United States Government caught all the poor old Apaches and moved them first to Florida, then to Alabama. Finally most of the tribe, at least the ones who had survived, ended up in Oklahoma; but my daddy's people, and Uncle Buddy Nock's, slipped away into the woods with some Choctaws and stayed in Alabama. The dark-skinned Nashes and Nocks intermarried with the pallid, cotton-haired Isbells, a dynastic farming family who may have invented the word "overpopulation."

One of my earliest memories, way back when I was

so little I was still wearing diapers pinned with two pins on each side and dragging an old baby blanket around everywhere I went, is when my daddy's two cousins came to live with us for a while. Their names were Henry Hope Nash and Harold Hope Nash. They were just a few years younger than my daddy, and even though they were twins you would never have guessed they were brothers by looking at them. They were both dark-skinned and tall, but Harold was big and heavy, with short thick black hair that he kept slicked back with hair oil. He had a big round face, and it seemed to me that he was always smiling. He talked with a loud booming voice that scared me, and it always seemed like he was too big for any room that he walked into.

Henry Hope was totally different from his brother. Henry Hope resembled my daddy, tall and thin, with a long thin face. But he always looked fragile and sad, and his eyes were pale and too big for his face. His hair, what there was of it, was long and straight, and the way it hung down around his face made him look pitiful somehow. He followed Harold around, his long arms dangling nervously at his sides, and his gawky hands plucking and fidgeting at his faded overalls and white shirts. His clothes were always starched and ironed so stiff that he appeared to be even thinner than he was.

So, when their mama and daddy, Aunt Lexie and Uncle Jim, were killed in Uncle Jim's logging truck, Harold and Henry Hope came to live with us for a while. I was so little then, but I can remember sitting on the floor playing with tinker toys with Henry Hope, while Harold laughed and sang crazy songs and ironed his brother's clothes with my mama's electric iron, which was plugged into an extension cord dangling from the ceiling light.

Harold sang lots of funny songs and one of them went like this:

> Has everybody heard about Henry?
> He's just come back from the army.
> Everybody knows he's back from the front.
> Hip-hip, hooray for Henry!

When he sang "Hip-hip hooray," Harold would slap his behind loudly, then wave his hand in the air. Henry Hope would duck his head sheepishly and smile, listening to his brother sing; but he never sang along.

"Sang that'n about the...tasty peanut," he'd drawl, and his face would light up as Harold launched into our favorite song.

> A man who has some good tasty peanuts
> And giveth his neighbor none
> The same shall have none of my tasty peanuts
> When his tasty peanuts are gone.
> Oh, won't it be joyful, joyful, joyful,
> Won't it be joyful, son.
> Oh won't it be joyful, joyful, joyful
> When his good tasty peanuts are gone.

> A man who has some soft sweet soda crackers
> And giveth his neighbor none
> The same shall have none of my soft sweet soda
> crackers
> When his soft sweet soda crackers are gone.
> Oh, won't it be joyful, joyful, joyful,

51

Won't it be joyful, son.
Oh, won't it be joyful, joyful, joyful,
When his soft sweet soda crackers are gone.

A man who has some good three dollar all wool
Plymouth Rock pants
And giveth his neighbor none
The same shall have none of my three dollar all
wool Plymouth Rock pants
When his three dollar all wool Plymouth Rock
pants are gone.
Oh, won't it be joyful, joyful, joyful,
Won't it be joyful, son.
Oh, won't it be joyful, joyful, joyful
When his good three dollar all wool Plymouth
Rock pants are gone.

As Harold sang, Henry Hope's eyes got wider and
wider and his smile got bigger and bigger, and after
Harold finished the song Henry Hope always nodded
his head and remarked, "I like that'n."

Mama and Daddy said Henry Hope was simple-
minded, like a child, but that was all right with me. As
years passed and Harold got a good job and bought a
little house in town for him and Henry Hope, they still
came to visit us sometimes. Harold would go out
drinking at night with Daddy and Uncle Buddy Nock;
but Henry Hope always stayed with Mama and me,
playing tinker toys even after I had stopped caring
anything about them. In the still, quiet night-time
house, Mama read out loud to us, from whatever book
she happened to be reading at the time, and Henry
Hope's face would have that far-away look. He'd stare
out the window into the dark night, and ask with his

strange halting voice,

"Cud'n Sara, when's them...boys...comin' home?"

He'd ask that same question over and over. But when he got too sleepy, he'd just lay down right on the floor and go to sleep.

That summer after we'd passed the third grade, when Willie T. and I were trying so hard to figure out the mystery of the map on Baby Junior's tongue, I guess I hadn't seen Harold and Henry Hope for at least a year. They usually came every Christmas, but Henry Hope had the flu that year, so they didn't come. I guess if they came any other time, it must have been while I was in school, because I hadn't seen them for a long time.

Then Daddy came home from work one afternoon, around the second week in June, and told us that Harold had been killed working on the railroad. Daddy said that two cars had coupled on him. That meant that two of the train cars had caught Harold between them when they were slamming together.

Willie T. came dragging mournfully across the yard and up onto our front porch. Mama patted Daddy gently on the back, and just said, "Well, Sam? Well, Sam?" and they both went into the house, crying. Willie T. and I just sat down on the front porch, and looked at each other for a long time without saying anything at all.

After a few minutes of silence Willie T. said, "That was Uncle Sam's cousin that got killed," as if he was telling me something I didn't already know. He huffed a couple of times and wiped his nose on the sleeve of his tee shirt, then continued; "Daddy came home and tole me and Mama about it. And Daddy said 'This'll break Sam Nash's heart.' Then Mama tole me to come up here to your house and stay while they went to the store."

Willie T. paused and poked around on the porch floor like he was trying to pick something out from between the wooden boards, then he said, "And Mama's gonna cook a lot of good food to bring to y'all tomorrow." He waited, looking at me, but when I didn't say anything he continued, speaking slowly and thoughtfully like he was remembering some almost forgotten details. "She said she was gonna make 'tater salad. And she's gonna make sweet p'tater pie. And chicken country captain! Just like Granny Rilla makes. And some rice, and...black-eye peas an' chow-chow. And...fried chicken. And fried chicken gizzards. And fried okry. And...butter beans, and cornbread. And pecan pralines! She really *did* say pecan pralines, and Daddy said he was gonna buy a bottle of whiskey."

I thought about Granny Rilla, and wished she was there with us, but she'd gone off to Tullahoma, Tennessee to spend the summer with one of her crazy old friends up north. I just sat there staring at my cousin, unable to speak. I felt just like you do at school when the teacher asks a question that you don't know the answer to. I even opened my mouth a little, and licked my lips, but I couldn't get any words to come out.

"You wanta go swing?" Willie T. asked, glancing across the yard at the long rope swing that Daddy had hung from a high limb, way up in our big hickory-nut tree.

I looked at the swing and thought about Henry Hope sitting there with a serious look on his face, his big gawky hands holding onto the ropes and his long legs stuck straight out in front of him. I remembered how he kept a determined look on his face, like he was working on something really important. And Harold stood on the front porch looking worried sometimes and smiling sometimes as he watched his brother in the swing. The limb was so high and the ropes were so long, the swing moved in a slow, high arc.

"You hold on tight, Henry Hope," Harold called. "Are you holding on?"

Henry Hope just looked more determined and kept swinging. I pushed him a little bit to keep him going good.

"Don't push him too high, baby," Harold cautioned. "Henry Hope, now you hold on."

Remembering that day, and how Harold had been so worried about his brother in the swing, I suddenly felt queasy and dizzy, and I leaned over just a little and threw up right on the porch.

Willie T. leaped up with a terrified look on his face, and ran to the screen door.

"Aunt Sara!" he yelled. "Come here quick, Aunt Sara, Lily C.'s puked on the porch!"

As I sat there on the wooden porch floor, feeling limp and dazed by the combination of summer heat and grief, I heard Mama rush out of the house repeating, "Oh, me. Oh, me." I felt her hands on both my arms as she lifted me to a semi-standing position. My legs wobbled lifelessly under me. As Mama wrapped one arm around my waist and lifted me off my feet, I looked out across the yard and saw someone approaching the house.

"Why, lookee yonder, Aunt Sara," Willie T. said softly. "It's Studebaker Freeman."

I watched the young black man striding briskly up

the dusty driveway, his back straight and his head held high, and his dark face and arms glistening in the bright sunlight. He was wearing suit pants and a white tee shirt with a pack of cigarettes rolled up in the left sleeve, and he was carrying an odd assortment of paper shopping bags and cardboard boxes of various sizes. We all knew that there was something funny about Studebaker carrying all those boxes and paper sacks all the time, 'cause they were usually empty, or maybe he'd have just one or two small things in one of the bags.

The way the story goes, Studebaker had wanted to become a doctor, and he got that idea from his old granddaddy. His granddaddy's name was Aloysius Freeman, but everybody way back in the old days just called him Wishes. He farmed a little piece of land on Moonlight Ridge and kept mostly to himself, but then when the flu epidemic came in 1918, Wishes Freeman took care of his own family and went all around town and out on the mountain from house to house, taking care of the sick folks and cooking pots of soup for people who were too sick to even find anything to eat. They say that nearly everybody in Eden got the flu, but because of Wishes taking care of everybody, only one person died, and that was the wife of a mean man who wouldn't let Wishes come in his house or even up on the porch to leave a pot of soup.

So Studebaker decided he wanted to be a doctor, and his rich brother, Ford Freeman, who was a lawyer in Louisiana, paid for him to go up north to medical school. Then after a little while, he went off to the war and he worked as a medic in the army. But one day without any warning, he just woke up crazy. Nobody claimed to know what had caused it, and Studebaker never told anybody what had happened. But he just came back home to Moonlight Ridge and never got to be a doctor. So every day, winter and summer, he walked around town talking to folks, sometimes talking to himself, and visiting people out on the mountain and occasionally diagnosing illnesses and giving out spontaneous medical advice.

My daddy said it was the war that made Studebaker crazy, all the killin' and sufferin' that he saw; and that he'd lost so many of his buddies, and now he was terrified of ever seeing another dead person. He said that Studebaker saw so many injured soldiers that he couldn't help, something had snapped inside his mind. Daddy said it was like Studebaker had lost some part of himself over there in the war, so there was an empty place somewhere inside him now.

It always seemed to me like he carried all those boxes and bags with him everywhere because of that empty place inside him, just 'cause it made him feel better to have something to hold onto, and not to be empty handed. He was just as friendly as anybody you'd ever want to see, but he could be snappy when he wanted to be, and everybody in Eden knew it was best not to tangle with him.

Katydids whirred incessantly around our yard in the summertime, getting louder and louder until it would just about bust your eardrums. As Studebaker passed my mama's rose bush, he shot a quick threatening glance at it, as if he resented the intrusion of the deafening noise and thought the rose bush might be the source of the screeching sound. He held a short stick in his right hand and whenever he walked around town, he used the stick to ward off any vicious or just curious dogs. The way he did that was just by pointing the stick at the dogs, and no matter how noisy or mean they were, the dogs would back off with their old tails between their legs, and leave him alone. Balancing all his shopping bags and cardboard boxes, he pointed the stick at the rose bush, then quickly shifted his attention to me and Mama and Willie T. Studebaker gave Willie T. a quick warning glance, then pointed at him with the short stick, which he wielded pretty much like a magic wand.

Willie T. looked up at my mother and grinned.

"Miss Nash," Studebaker said, "I've come to offer my condolences to you and Mr. Nash on your recent tragic bereavement."

"Not now, Studebaker, not now," Mama replied, stepping gingerly around the mess I had made.

Daddy came out onto the porch. He was holding his big white handkerchief wadded in his hand, and his nose looked red and moist. He pushed the handkerchief into his pocket and stepped closer to the black man.

"Mr. Nash," Studebaker announced formally, "I've come to offer my condolences to *you* on your recent tragic bereavement." Saying this, he cut his eyes around and looked straight at my mother.

"Well, thank you for coming, Stu," my daddy replied. His voice was low and a little shaky sounding. He reached out and shook hands with the visitor.

Mama started toward the door, still dangling me in the air like a Raggedy Ann doll.

"I can walk now, Mama," I whispered.

"Is *she* sick?" Studebaker Freeman asked as he watched me closely.

"She's just a little upset, that's all," Mama answered. "And it's just so hot . . ."

"*Hot*? I know that's right!" Studebaker exclaimed. "Yes it is, *so* hot! Here, this will help her. She just needs a little tonic. All this trouble and in this hot weather, too!" As he spoke, he was digging around in one of his shopping bags, and he pulled out a Buffalo Rock ginger ale. "Here, this is what she needs. You got ice?"

Willie T. giggled, and Stu pointed at him with his magic stick, then he pulled another Buffalo Rock out of his sack.

"Here, you better give some to that boy, too. Don't want no more sick childrens in this heat."

"Well, that's real nice," Mama said, trying to smile. "Thank you, Studebaker. Y'all tell him thank you."

"Thank you, Studebaker," I said.

"Thank you, Studebaker Freeman," Willie T. chanted in a high-pitched, singsong voice.

As Willie T., Mama, and I went into the house, I heard our visitor talking to Daddy on the front porch.

"Now, Mr. Nash, you know my brother is a successful attorney in New Orleans, and if any legal problems should arise up out of this, you need to let him know. He'll be able to help you with any legal questions and you know, it's the truth, with the Railroad you never know what can happen, and you sure better get your hose pipe and wash this porch off now. Um-hm, it's *so* hot out here. It sure is. You have to watch your childrens in this kind of heat because they can dehydrate. Um-hmm, dehydrate, that is sure enough the truth."

While Willie T., Mama, and I sat at the kitchen table drinking the peppery ginger ale out of ice-filled jelly glasses, we could hear Daddy spraying water on the front porch while Stu chattered away. Every once in a while Daddy would say something in his low, soft voice. It was hard to tell what they were saying, but they stayed out there on the porch and talked for a long time. After a while, Daddy came into the kitchen and sat down wearily at the table.

"Is he gone?" Mama whispered.

"Um-hmm," Daddy answered, shaking his head. "He sure likes to talk!"

"I never know what to think of him," Mama said. "He's crazy as a bessie-bug!"

"Well, he's a little peculiar, I guess," Daddy agreed. "He's got his own ways, too. But he's so kind-hearted, you can't help but like him."

Just then, Willie T. burped so loud that me and Mama and Daddy just about jumped out of our skin.

"Oh, for goodness sakes! Willie T. Nock!" Mama scolded.

"It's that Buff'ler Rock, Aunt Sara," Willie T. pleaded. "It ain't *my* fault!"

Nobody ate supper that afternoon. We just sat around the table and looked at the cornbread and pinto beans and mustard greens cooling in the bowls. Aunt Rachel and Uncle Buddy Nock came by for a little while. Daddy and Uncle Buddy stepped out on the back porch and Aunt Rachel looked at the untouched food on the table. She told Mama not to worry with cooking for the next few days, that she was planning on cooking enough for everybody. Then she and Uncle Buddy left, leaving Willie T. with us.

After we finally gave up on supper, Willie T. and I trailed off down toward the Howards'. We didn't say a word; we just ambled drearily down the road. A little wind picked up, and off in the distance we could see lightning; the kind Mama called heat lightning, and the trees and bushes rustled around us as we walked.

When we arrived at Estaleen's house, we heard soft music, sort of sad sounding, and we crept up onto the porch and peeped in the open door. We could see straight through the small living room into the kitchen where Estaleen sat at the little old wooden table, surrounded by all different colors of crepe paper. She was crying and making paper flowers. Every once in a while she'd wipe tears off her cheeks with the back of her hand; then she glanced up and saw us standing at the door.

She stood up slowly and walked to the screen door without saying a word. She just held the screen open for us to come in. The song on the radio was turned down low, I expect so it wouldn't wake up the baby.

And then Estaleen did the strangest thing. She said real soft, and I could hear tears in her voice, "Daince with me, Lily C." And she held out her arms to me just like a little child. Willie T. stood with one foot on top of the other, watching us with the slightest hint of a puzzled smile on his face, as Estaleen and I danced a slow box step around her little kitchen. We turned, so that Estaleen's back was to the door, and that's when I saw Cowboy standing in the doorway behind Willie T., leaning with his arm up on the door frame, watching us. I've never seen a face look any sadder, and that's when it came to me that Estaleen and Cowboy really loved Harold the same way we all did.

Cowboy put his hand real easy on Willie T.'s shoulder and watched me and Estaleen dancing to that sad drifting music. Then he came up real quietly and took Estaleen in his old long arms, and the two of them just went right on dancing right where I had left off. Willie T. and I watched for just a minute, then we slipped out of the house and walked back home. The sun had gone down, but it was still not all the way dark, and we made our way along the shadowy road back home without saying a word. It just didn't seem like there was anything to say.

Six

The Funeral

Moonlight Ridge Baptist Church sits on one side of the mountain road, and the Moonlight Ridge Cemetery is at the end of a narrow dirt driveway on the other side of the road. The cemetery is surrounded by thickets of blackberry bushes, honeysuckle vines, dogwood trees, and sweet-gum trees. I guess there are a few people buried there that are not related to us, but most of them are. Some of the tombstones are so old you can't read the names on them; but there are plenty of Greenberrys, Leverts, Nashes and Nocks. And Isbells? There's boocoos of them!

The cemetery is so far off the main road that you never hear any cars or trucks passing by, and when you're there in the graveyard it's so quiet, when nobody's talking all you hear is the sound of birds and katydids. The day of Harold's funeral was scorching hot, and everybody was quiet, standing in the bright sweltering sun. When anyone whispered or coughed, it sounded really loud.

Henry Hope stood beside me with both his hands clasped real tight in front of him. Sometimes he'd look at my daddy, like he was watching to see how to stand and what to do.

There was a new young preacher, Brother Goforth, who had only been at Moonlight Ridge Church just a few weeks. He stood in front of us, beside Harold's casket in the glaring sunshine, wearing black pants and a white short-sleeved shirt, holding his black Bible. His face looked stricken and sad, like he had lost a member of his own family, and he looked for the world like he was trying to come up with something to say.

"This is a sad day," Brother Goforth finally announced softly, sounding a little puzzled. For a while, it seemed like that was all he intended to say about it, and everybody just stood there looking at him, waiting. Then he continued, "I didn't know Harold Nash...I'd never met him. Never saw him in church. But, I've been told that he was a good, kind man, and I believe it's so. I see he's left many a grievin' heart here today...family and friends. And his best friend of all, Mr. Henry Hope Nash, here."

Henry Hope jerked slightly when he heard his name spoken, like you'll do when the teacher calls your name at school. He looked down at me and I looked up at him, and at that very moment I knew he was listening to a strange, tinny, mewing sound that I could hear starting up somewhere at the back of the graveyard.

"I'd like to read from the book of St. John, chapter fourteen," the young preacher told us. " 'Let not your heart be troubled,' our Lord Jesus said. 'In my Father's house are many mansions. If it were not so, I would have told you.' "

"Amen," a few of the older men called out. "Amen, Brother."

Somewhere in the distance, the high-pitched sound started up again, like someone humming in a high, squeaky voice. I saw Henry Hope look out across the crowd, then he looked down at me again.

"Then our Lord said, 'I go to prepare a place for you,' " the preacher continued. " 'That where I am, there ye may be also.' "

"Amen. Amen, Brother," the men responded.

Brother Goforth looked sincerely at the many faces in front of him and said, "I believe Harold Hope Nash is in that place today, that place prepared for him by our Lord."

This time the squeaky sound was closer, right in the middle of the crowd, and getting louder. I listened, thinking that it sounded almost like short, quick notes of music from a fiddle. But not really a tune, just a series of notes.

People in the crowd started shuffling around, moving their feet and whispering a little. I saw a couple of people nudging the ones next to them and looking at each other with puzzled expressions on their faces. Brother Goforth continued.

" 'And whither I go ye know, and the way ye know.' Jesus said, 'I am the way, the truth, and the light.' "

"There!" my daddy suddenly called out, interrupting the preacher, and I knew that he had heard the squeaky noise, too. He looked all around above the heads of all the folks standing there, like he was trying to see where that sound was coming from.

At this point, the whining, singing noise was really loud, and the crowd of people parted, making a clear path straight up to the preacher and Harold's flower-covered casket. Henry Hope touched my shoulder softly and we both leaned forward a little, looking for the source of the high-pitched squeaking sound.

Just then I heard Willie T. behind me whispering loudly, "The lord! Look, Lily C. It's a possum!"

Now possums are usually nocturnal; that means they mostly come out at night-time. But if they get disturbed or curious about what's going on, they'll come out in the day-time. And sure enough, as we all watched, a mama possum with a bunch of little baby possums hanging onto her back, waddled out of the crowd and headed straight for Harold's casket. The mama possum was big and gray with a white face, black ears, and a long pink tail dragging the ground behind her. All the baby possums were little and gray with white faces and white ears that were ruffled around the edges. They had little pink tails, tiny pink hands, and tiny black shining eyes. As she waddled along, the mama possum made soft little smacking noises; but the baby possums were *singing*. It was the prettiest, sweetest sound I had ever heard; sweet high-pitched notes of music.

The astonished preacher stared at the possums with a worried look on his face. He stood with his mouth open, and I thought it looked like he was trying to catch his breath, like a fish out of water.

The possums got louder.

Everyone in the crowd looked astounded and confused, and I felt afraid that someone might hurt the mama possum and her babies, trying to run them away from the funeral. Then I heard Henry Hope's voice.

"Them possums...are...singin' to my brother."

My breath caught in my throat, and sudden tears filled my eyes. The preacher remained standing with his mouth open, looking at the singing possums.

The mama possum seemed to settle down right in front of us all, and she started grooming herself, licking one front paw, which really looked like a funny little hand, then wiping and combing her gray fur. The baby possums kept singing. When one fell off the mama's back, his squeaky song stopped abruptly till he managed to climb back on, then he joined back in with the others.

Gradually, I began to hear a melody, just a slight pattern of a tune, up and down, up and down. Dah-da-dah, dah-da-dah. At the front of a crowd of people over to my right, Estaleen Howard was standing with Cowboy. She had a red crepe-paper flower in her hair, tucked behind her ear, and Cowboy had a white one stuck in the top button-hole of his faded shirt. Somehow the sight of them looking so sad with their crepe-paper flowers just about broke my heart. Estaleen was holding baby Junior against her shoulder and he was bouncing up and down like some kind of a wind-up toy, in time with the possum singing. Very softly, in a clear gentle voice, Estaleen began to sing, almost like the words came unconsciously, like someone talking to herself.

Trouble and trials often betray those
On in the weary body to stray.

The words matched exactly with the rhythm of the sounds the possums were making.

Other voices joined in immediately, and I heard my daddy's soft deep voice as the crowd sang the lyrics with Estaleen's clear voice leading them.

But we shall walk beside the still waters
With the Good Shepherd leading the way.

Those who have strayed were
 Sought by the Master
He who once gave his life for the sheep.
Out on the mountain, still he is searching
Bringing them in forever to keep.

Going up home to live in green pastures
Where we shall live and die nevermore.
Even the Lord will be in that number
When we shall reach that Heavenly shore.

We will not heed the voice of a stranger
For he would lead us all to despair.
Following on with Jesus our savior
We shall all reach that country so fair.

Going up home to live in green pastures
Where we shall live and die nevermore.
Even the Lord will be in that number
When we shall reach that Heavenly shore.

With the last word of the song, everybody fell totally silent. The baby in Estaleen's arms stopped jumping up and down, and the mama possum stopped grooming herself and looked at the crowd for the first time.

Everybody stared at the possum, and the possum stared at us.

Someone stepped forward out of the crowd and softly approached the possums. It was Studebaker Freeman.

"Get from here!" he whispered, stomping his foot in the hot dust. "Get from here!"

With Stu walking close behind her and pointing with his magic stick, the possum obediently waddled past the casket, past the preacher, and made her way toward the bushes at the edge of the graveyard.

"Um-hm. Um-hmm," Studebaker hummed as the baby possums continued to sing their squeaky sweet notes. "Um-hm, that's real fine, but you got to get on away from here, 'less you want to end up on a plank with some sweet potatoes before you know it!"

My mother had stood absolutely still during the entire possum cantata, with a serious and sort of puzzled expression on her face like she always has in church. I heard Daddy take a deep breath after all that singing, and when the possums had disappeared into the woods he looked at me and then at Henry Hope, and just said, "Well, I'll say!"

Stu returned, looking official and business-like, and stood at the back of the crowd where he had left his bunch of cardboard boxes and shopping bags all piled on the ground.

Brother Goforth cleared his throat a few times and finally regained his voice, then said, "You know, brothers and sisters, the Bible says that the Lord shall use foolish things to confound the wise,"

"Amen! Um-hm! I know that's the truth. He *will* do that!" Studebaker called out from the back of the crowd.

The older men all turned and looked at Studebaker, then turned back toward the preacher and said "Amen. Amen, Brother!" not wanting to be outdone.

Then Brother Goforth ended Harold's funeral

service by saying, "In the scripture the Lord tells us, 'These things I have spoken unto you, that in me ye might have peace.' "

"Mr. Preacher," Henry Hope spoke up. "I think my brother is...up in Heaven now."

"I think so, too," the preacher said. "I think so, too." Then he walked over to Henry Hope and put both arms around his neck and hugged him.

Standing behind me, Willie T. had calmly started talking in tongues.

The new preacher was proud and stunned when several people got converted that day and asked to join the church. I guess it just goes to show you. Most everybody there lined up to shake Henry Hope's hand and pat him on the back, and he shyly allowed them to do so. Then the crowd broke up, shaking hands with each other and patting each other on the back. The men removed their hats and wiped their sweaty foreheads with handkerchiefs, and the women fanned themselves with their Sunday hats. We took Henry Hope with us and went to our house to get out of the blazing heat.

When Mama, Daddy, Henry Hope, and I got home, Mama put quilts and pillows and an electric fan on the shady front porch, and we all gratefully collapsed onto the cool soft pallets to take a nap. When I woke up it was night-time. I could hear Bu, the hoot-owl, calling in the dark, and Henry Hope was sitting up in one of the front-porch rocking chairs, humming the same haunting tune we had heard the possums sing.

I climbed onto his lap and leaned my head against his heart; Henry Hope laid his wet cheek against the top of my head, and we listened to the hoot-owl calling in the dark.

Seven

Another Disaster

Mama and Daddy worried about Henry Hope staying by himself, so sometimes he spent the night with us. He'd spend the long hot summer days sitting on the front porch helping Mama shell peas, humming tunelessly to himself; and then he'd spend the long dark summer evenings on the front porch with Daddy, listening to baseball games and boxing on the radio. But he seemed restless and always wanted to go back to his own little house where he and his brother had lived together so happily.

"Now Cud'n Sara, I just have to...go see about my...house. I need to watch out...for turn-mites, just like my brother Harold...told me. If they take hold... they'll eat up your sub-floorin', and your two-by-fours, and your roofin'...trusses. They eat...wood."

So, Mama let him go. He seemed to get along fine by himself, much to everybody's surprise. Whenever Henry Hope was at home by himself, Daddy would stop by every day on his way home from work just to make sure there was good food in the house and things weren't in too big a mess.

Mama gave him one of our orange kittens to keep him company, and he named it Shoo-fly.

I had other things to worry about. Two days after the fourth of July, Willie T. came down with the whooping cough.

The fourth of July was my daddy's birthday and he always cooked barbecue out in the back yard on a brick barbecue pit he had built under a huge sweet-gum tree. He wouldn't use any kind of wood for the fire except hickory, and he cooked up his own secret recipe of barbecue sauce in an old beat-up pan. He wrapped a piece of white cotton cloth around one end of a short hickory stick, and that's what he used to swab the barbecue sauce onto the ribs over the fire. The smell was tantalizing as he slow-cooked the ribs over the hot coals, and the results were always mouth-watering delicious. We had a beautiful green watermelon, and Daddy had already laid a broom straw across its middle to make sure it was ripe, and I had watched in awe as the straw turned, quickly lining up vertically on the huge melon. When Daddy cut it open with the big butcher knife, it was so red and ripe inside, it popped open with a loud cracking sound, and the air was filled with the luscious sweet smell.

Aunt Rachel, Uncle Buddy Nock, and Willie T. had come to eat Fourth-of-July barbecue with us, then while the grown-ups talked and played cards, Willie T. and I wandered down the road toward Estaleen and Cowboy's house. We stopped in the curve of the road and sat on the ground under the persimmon tree because the sun was so hot on the dusty unpaved road.

"You still got the map?" Willie T. asked as we sat in a shady spot under the little tree. He was running his fingers through the grass and moss on the ground.

Every once in a while he'd look at a pebble or some little thing he'd found, then run his fingers through the grass some more.

"It's home in my dresser drawer," I answered drowsily. I watched my cousin chewing thoughtfully on a blade of green grass he had pulled and stuck in his mouth.

"You wanta go lookin'?" he asked, then turned his head and spit out the piece of chewed-up grass.

Willie T. had sweat and dirt on his face and barbecue sauce on his shirt. He rubbed his grimy hand across his face, smearing a little more dirt on his sunburned cheeks.

"It's too hot," I answered. "We'll have to go early one mornin', right after breakfast before it gets too hot."

"Yeah," he agreed. "It's purty hot, all right. Hotter'n a he-haint in torment! It wuz so hot yesterday, I seen a red-bird sittin' on a limb fannin' his-self with his wing."

"Really?"

"Yeah. And it wuz so hot day before yesterday, I seen a jay-bird sprayin' his-self with the hose pipe in our back yard!"

"Willie T.! You did not!" I protested, glaring at him.

"Uh-huh! I shore did. And the day before day before yesterday, I seen a buzzard wearin' sunglasses and a straw hat..."

I punched Willie T. on the shoulder just about as hard as I could, jarring him a little and interrupting his tale momentarily.

"Ouch! Dammit...and a bathing suit," he continued while rubbing his arm briskly. "And he was settin' right under this here tree drinkin' a great big Grapico."

"No you didn't. You didn't see any such thing! You're just tryin' yourself, and you know it!"

"Shore did. And the day *before* the day before the day...wait a minute. How many days did I already say?"

At that point, Willie T. burst into a noisy fit of laughing and giggling and started rolling around on the ground. His sunburned face got redder and redder as he lost his breath from laughing so hard. His fits of laughter, and the thought of that buzzard in sunglasses drinking a Grapico, caused my giggle-box to turn over and I started laughing as hard as my wriggling cousin. I tried to grab ahold of him to make him sit up, but he was rolling around and laughing so hard, I couldn't get a good grip on him.

"And that other day before that *other* day," he gasped, "it was another bird, sittin' in the willer tree, shavin' his self with a safety razor, and singin' 'Shave and a haircut, six bits!' "

"You're tellin' a big fib, and you know it!" I scolded, barely able to speak. I had laughed until I had tears running down my face as my crazy cousin rolled on the ground, kicking and gasping for breath, telling one big lie after another.

"He shore did. And then he had just one feather left, right on the top of his head, and he squirted Brylcreem on it and started singin', 'Brylcreem, a little dab'll do ya!' "

"Willie T. Nock, you're puttin' on, and you know it! You got to stop it," I pleaded, wiping tears from my

74

eyes. I was used to him telling silly stories all the time; he had his own private version of The Gingerbread Boy that involved the Gingerbread Boy running through town and eating up old men, old women, children, dogs, cats, sacks of oranges, and fried chicken gizzards by the score. But normally he always kept a straight face, trying to make me believe he was telling the truth. I had never seen him this hysterical. We were both sobbing and crying and laughing, all at the same time.

Then gradually Willie T. got control of himself, and he lay on the ground panting, "Oh, lordy. Oh, lordy." till he finally calmed down and his breathing started to become normal. He squirmed around on his back like a wiggle worm, wiping his eyes with both hands.

A few seconds of silence passed, then he grinned at me and sang, "A little dab'll do ya!", and we both broke out laughing again.

This could have gone on forever, I guess, but from the distance we heard Aunt Rachel calling, "William! Will-yum!"

We struggled to our feet, holding onto each other, barely able to walk back to the house after all the laughing and crying. Nobody in the world can make up silly stories like Willie T. Nock.

It was just two days later, Mama told me that Aunt Rachel had to carry Willie T. to the doctor because he'd coughed for two days and nights without stopping. Dr. Carlisle had gone off to Lake Talquin in Quincy, Florida on a fishin' trip, and old Dr. Driggers told Aunt Rachel it was sure enough the whooping cough. Mama also told me that the Nock house had to be quarantined so nobody else could catch it, and so I couldn't go to see Willie T. But I sneaked off and went anyway.

When I got to their house, I saw Aunt Rachel

75

before she could see me. She was sitting on her front porch in a rocking chair, fanning herself with a McCall's magazine and smoking a cigarette. Her long brown hair, permed into a frizzy mess from a recent Tony Home Permanent, was pulled into a ponytail on the right side of her head, making her look sort of like a cocker spaniel with only one big curly ear.

I stopped at the mailbox and ducked around the edge of the yard behind a row of wild untrimmed hedge bushes. Every year in the spring, those bushes were full of sweet-smelling little white blossoms, but now, in the heavy heat of summer, they were no longer blooming. Aunt Rachel had one big althea bush, right up beside the front porch, full of big purple blooms, but there were no other flowers in the yard because of Willie T.'s allergies. He was always sneezing and itching with the nettle rash.

Just as I got close to the back of the little white house, Aunt Rachel's voice startled me as she called from the front porch, "Now, William, you quit that singing. You're gonna make yourself start coughing again."

Standing still against the white shingled wall, I heard Willie T.'s voice, weakly singing along with the radio playing in the kitchen. The song on the radio was Hank Williams singing "Your Cheatin' Heart," and Willie T.'s voice actually sounded pretty good, for somebody with the whooping cough. But then, about halfway through the mournful song, he suddenly started coughing really loud, making strange whistling noises with every violent cough.

I climbed up onto a large brown butter churn that was sitting upside-down just below the bedroom window. His bed was right beside the open window and, looking in as I leaned over the windowsill, I saw my poor cousin thrashing around and kicking the white bed sheets as he coughed and whooped.

"Willie T., are you all right?"

He looked up at me with panicky, watery eyes, his mouth open in the shape of a big "O" as he gasped for air, then erupted into another long fit of coughing.

After about a minute of hacking and thrashing his arms and legs like a maniac, the coughing fit subsided and he collapsed, limp and pathetic on the untidy bed. His face was flushed and sweaty, and he gazed at me pitifully.

"Oh Lily C., I'm dyin', sure as the world," he moaned. Then he coughed another couple of weak-sounding coughs. "And you ain't 'spose to be here. Really, you ort to stay away, 'cause you could catch it from me and. . ."

Just then, Aunt Rachel walked into the bedroom, still fanning herself with the magazine.

"Lily Claire! I'll swear to my time!" she exclaimed, waving the McCall's at me like she was trying to sweep me away. "You get away from that window! If you catch this whoopin' cough, your mama will kill me! You get home, young lady! Go on. Get away from here right this minute!"

Willie T. was starting to cough again, and I turned to jump off the upside-down churn. The churn turned over as I jumped, and I fell to the ground, scraping my knee and hitting my elbow on the heavy brown pottery churn.

"Oh, oh, oh," I moaned as the miserable tingling of a bumped funny-bone shot up my arm. Rubbing my elbow frantically, I trotted away from the house, followed by the sounds of my poor cousin's spasmodic

77

coughing.

As I ran down the hill and headed for home, the little wisp of smoke in the distance was barely visible. Although it was summer and all the trees were full of green leaves, I automatically thought, "Somebody must be burning leaves."

When I got home, I was so worried about Willie T., I couldn't do anything but cry and mope. Mama didn't say anything about where I'd been; she just asked me if I wanted to play Chinese checkers, and I dozed off in the middle of the game, crumpled up in the big easy chair in our living room.

I woke up gradually, drifting in and out of sleep, the afternoon heat on me like a heavy wool blanket. My mouth was dry and I drowsily tried to remember the last time I'd had a drink of water.

"Mama," I mumbled, wanting to ask for a glass of water. But my lips barely moved and my voice didn't work right because my mouth and throat were so dry.

My eyelids were heavy and hard to open, but finally I was able to focus my eyes on my mama. She was standing at the screen door with her back to me. She was talking to someone standing on the other side of the screen, and as I became fully awake I saw the uniform and heard the gravelly voice, and I recognized Clyde Tucker, the chief of police.

My mother's hand was on the screen door, as if she intended to keep the tall, pot-bellied policeman out of her house.

"Well, Clyde, she's been right there asleep in that chair all afternoon, right there where she is now," Mama said.

Officer Clyde Tucker leaned a little to one side so he could get a better look at me, I guess. He looked right at me, his forehead wrinkled under the bill of his policeman's cap.

"Don't your sister have a little boy about that same age?" he asked, leaning a little further, his fat red face right up against the screen.

"My sister's little boy is quarantined with the whooping cough! Clyde Tucker, don't you come around here asking questions about our children! It sounds like you've got plenty to keep you busy without scaring our children to death. What in the world made you come here asking questions?"

The chief of police snatched his policeman's cap off his sweaty head and slapped it noisily against his pants leg.

"That Howard gal is layin' at the hospital near dead with the smoke inhalation. Says she left her old 'lectric iron plugged into the overhead light socket, then she went outside to hang out some sheets on the clothesline, and she set down under the tree and went to sleep in the shade. And that's when the fire started. Says she knows she went back inside to get the baby, but that's all she can remember. And she's screamin' and cryin' and talkin' some crazy tale about your younguns hangin' around her baby all the time. And Cowboy Howard's gone plumb wild! I'll tell you what, Cowboy would be right here right now his-self, but he cain't leave that gal's bedside for a second. They're both cryin' and carryin' on like crazy people! What you want me to do? I got to talk to your little girl and your sister's boy, too!"

Chief of Police Tucker kept bobbing and swaying, trying to get a better look at me through the screen door. I chose to lie still in the big chair, pretending to be asleep with my eyes open, getting more and more frightened by what he was saying.

"Well, you better go looking for that baby and quit messing around here, wasting time! I can assure you that, for all intents and purposes, Lily Claire has been right there asleep all afternoon and doesn't know anything about it."

Tucker squinched up his eyebrows and reared his head back, looking down his long sweaty nose at my mama.

"Intents and purposes? Now, what the Hell does *that* mean?"

"Well, Clyde," Mama answered patiently, "it means if she says anything, I'll let you know. And furthermore, I'd advise you not to go bothering Rachel about all this. She's high strung."

"Well, I'll be damned!" the police chief sputtered, slapping his cap against his leg again. Then he turned and stepped off the high end of the porch, where the steps weren't, and plunged out of sight, landing right in the middle of a mess of hydrangea bushes. Mama turned around toward me with both hands over her face, shaking her head and trying to hold back a laugh.

"Lord, lord," she sighed. "My hydrangeas!"

"Mama, what in the world has happened while I've been asleep?" I asked her. I could hear Police Chief Tucker's tires slinging gravel as he drove, a little too fast, away from our yard.

"Well, Honey, he says that the Howard's house has burned down and . . ."

"Oh, Mama! No!" I sobbed. I felt like the breath had been knocked out of my lungs and my heart started racing like I'd been running up a hill. I jumped up from the chair, tears stinging my eyes. "Oh, no," I cried. "What's happened to Estaleen and Baby Junior?"

"Well, Estaleen's at the hospital, and nobody really knows where the baby is. Did you see anything this morning? Where did you go, anyway?"

"Oh, Mama!" I gasped, remembering the smoke I had seen as I left Aunt Rachel's house. "I think maybe I saw some smoke! Estaleen's house must have been on fire then, and I saw the smoke and didn't even know! I went to look at Willie T. through the window, and I saw the smoke on the way home after Aunt Rachel ran me off."

"And you didn't go to the Howard's today?"

"No, ma'am. I was so worried about Willie T." I paused, feeling panicky and sick. "What can we do?"

"Lily Claire, right now I don't know anything we *can* do. Clyde says he's almost sure the baby wasn't in the house. He talked like he thinks somebody kidnapped that baby ... or at least, that's what Estaleen thinks. But who would do such a terrible thing? Who would *want* Estaleen Howard's baby?"

I was busy putting on my sandals that I had slipped off earlier while we were playing Chinese checkers, and my mind was racing, trying to think of something to do.

"I sure hope something bad hasn't happened to Estaleen's baby," Mama said, shaking her head sadly. "The way Clyde said they were carrying on at the hospital! To lose a child is the worst thing that can happen to anybody."

Mama walked to the front door and stood, looking through the screen.

"Didn't Rachel tell me that baby had a map on its tongue? Isn't that the craziest thing you ever heard? That's what you call an old wives tale, Lily Claire."

"It's true, Mama. Junior does have a map on his

tongue. And Aunt Rachel told Willie T. that a baby with a map on its tongue will die."

Mama didn't say anything, so I moved closer to her and took her hand in mine.

"It's not true, is it, Mama?"

"Hm," Mama replied softly, like she was thinking about something but didn't want to say anything else.

After a while she said, "Well, well, well. I've got to get supper ready. Your Daddy will be home in a little while. Turnip greens are done. I'll just fix us some cornbread and iced tea. Sounds good, doesn't it?"

"Yes'm," I answered, but I was still thinking about Baby Junior. "Mama, have you ever seen a treasure map?"

"A treasure map? Huh! Well, I don't know. In a book maybe. What made you think of that?"

"Well, just what can you find with a treasure map if you had one? Is it like a pot a' gold at the end of a rainbow, or what?"

Mama laughed and ran her fingers through my hair, pushing it back away from my face. "Lily Claire, you ask the funniest questions sometimes. I guess there's all sorts of treasure; maybe a different kind of treasure for every map. I guess if you had a treasure map, there's no telling what you could find." Mama took the barrette out of my hair, then put it back in again. It just seems like a barrette is one thing that's never in the right place, as far as my mama is concerned.

"Come on, now," she said, giving my hair one more firm pat, "and help me get supper ready. You can cut up a lemon for the tea."

When Daddy got home, Mama told him all about Estaleen's house burning down and Junior disappearing and Police Chief Tucker falling off the front porch into the hydrangea bushes. I ate slowly, listening to my parents talking about all the house fires they had ever seen or heard about, and every disappeared person they'd ever known of. They talked for a while about the poor little Lindbergh baby that was kidnapped, which of course I knew all about, after listening to Miss Tweedy reciting the complete history of the United States for a whole entire year.

When we all had finished eating, Daddy pushed his chair back away from the table and stretched his long legs out in front of him, arms crossed over his chest.

"Has Henry Hope been here today?" he asked.

Mama said no, he hadn't, and Daddy said Henry Hope wasn't at home when he'd stopped by there after work.

"He goes off fishin' with Studebaker ever' once in a while," Daddy chuckled. "Now, don't you bet they're a pair!"

Mama and Daddy sat at the table, talking and laughing, and I went into my bedroom and lay across my bed. The sun was just going down, and it burned bright red through my window and across the Drunkard's Path quilt that Granny Rilla had made for me. I took the map out of the drawer beside my bed and studied it for a while, running my finger over the wrinkled paper, tracing the black pencil lines that curved and curled across the page. I kept remembering what Mama had said; a different kind of treasure for every map, and I wished Willie T. was there to help me figure things out.

When I woke up the next morning, I knew what I had to do.

Eight

The Search

The next day was Saturday, and Daddy got up early and went into town by himself. I was just finishing my breakfast when I heard his old black pickup truck slide into the yard. A second later, I heard his truck door slam. A second later, he loped into the house and the screen door slammed behind him as he rushed into the kitchen.

"Sara, go get ready to go to town. We're goin' to the hospital. I think you'd better talk to Estaleen and Cowboy."

Mama frowned and squinched her eyebrows together. "Sam, do you think that's a good idea?"

"I believe we better. Those two are out of their minds, wantin' to find their baby. It's the awfullest mess you've ever seen. And pore Estaleen is layin' there on the bed... They've give her something to knock her out, but she's fightin' it and won't go to sleep. She's just layin' there with her eyes shut, runnin' her hands back and forth across the bedsheets and saying, 'I ain't asleep yit. I ain't asleep yit.' "

"Oh, Sam," Mama moaned.

"And I can tell Cowboy's got one of his headaches," Daddy continued. "His face is as white as the bedsheet. But he won't say anything about it. And you won't believe it, Clyde's got *Stu* locked up in the jail accused of kidnappin' that baby. Seems like somebody saw Stu carryin' all those boxes and things, and they figured he could have carried that baby off inside of one of the boxes! So Clyde just went and picked him up, just like that!" Daddy snapped his fingers loudly.

Mama gasped and put both her hands over her mouth, staring at Daddy as he continued talking.

"And Clyde says they're fixin' to transfer Stu to the jail in Birmingham, because Oley Hutchins has done got his Ku Klux buddies mixed up in it, so Clyde wants to get Stu away from here."

Mama let out a little whimper like she'd stumped her toe.

"This is bad," she said, and started grabbing dirty dishes off the table.

"And now Henry Hope's disappeared!" Daddy added, throwing his hands up in the air.

"Disappeared?" Mama repeated like she wasn't sure she'd heard right. "Well, where could *he* be?"

"Lord, I don't know. I tried to talk to Stu at the jail, but couldn't get much sense out of him. Somethin' about Henry Hope's kitten running off and they were tryin' to find it. But mostly he was cussin' Clyde Tucker!"

"Studebaker? Cussing?" Mama dropped the dirty plates into the sink and stared at Daddy as if she thought he was making up this whole story.

"You better believe it! Up one side and down the other! Clyde threw all Stu's mess out into the alley, and

85

Stu's as mad as Hell. Here, I picked this up."

Daddy held out his hand, and he was holding Studebaker Freeman's magic stick. I reached out to touch it, and he thrust it into my hand, then absent-mindedly wiped his hand on his trousers leg.

I held the magic stick up close to my face, feeling a little nervous, looking at it like it was made out of pure gold. My parents rushed around for a few minutes, then they were about to leave to go to town, and I was still standing in the same spot, looking at the stick.

"Lily Claire, I'm gonna let you stay here," Mama told me as she followed Daddy out the front door. "Stay inside, you hear me?"

The screen door slammed, then I heard Daddy's truck start up.

I was too preoccupied to pay them much attention. I ran my hand along the magic stick, then held it out in front of me and waved it cautiously a few times. Nothing happened.

"Willie T.," I whispered.

When I got to their house, Aunt Rachel and Uncle Buddy were nowhere around. The little white house looked deserted, but when I got closer, I could hear the radio playing softly in the kitchen. I went straight to Willie T.'s window and set the turned-over churn up. I had to lay the magic stick on the ground and use both hands to turn the heavy churn upside down, then I picked up the stick and climbed up to the window.

My pitiful cousin lay flat on his back with both arms and legs thrown out like a big X on the rumpled sheets. A pillow in a wrinkled white pillowcase was on the floor at the foot of the bed. When he breathed, he made a sharp screeching squeak, like when you stretch the end of a balloon and let air escape in little spurts.

"Willie T., Willie T., wake up, we have to…"

The noisy breathing abruptly turned into a loud honk, and Willie T. opened his eyes. Just like in a movie, he looked all around the room, wiped his hand across his face, and said, "How long have I been asleep?"

"Don't you remember? You've got the whooping cough. You've been sick, but you've got to get up now. Everything's in a terrible mess. The Howards' house has burned down and Junior's disappeared and Estaleen's in the hospital and look!" I leaned over the windowsill. "I've got Studebaker Freeman's magic stick, so we have to take the map and follow it to find out where Baby Junior is."

"The map?" Willie T. asked, looking at me like he was trying to put two and two together.

"Yes, the *map*," I insisted.

For a few seconds Willie T. didn't move. He looked at the stick that I was holding right in front of his nose, then he looked at me.

"How'd you get that?" His voice was raspy, like when you have a sore throat.

"Oh, Willie T., Studebaker's in jail, they think he kidnapped the baby, and that awful old Clyde Tucker threw all his things out in the alley. Daddy picked this up and brought it home."

"Oh."

"And to make things worse, they're takin' Studebaker to the Birmingham jail to get away from the Ku Kluxes. You got to get up. Can you get up?" I asked him.

"Uh, I thank I can," he wheezed. "Ku Kluxes?"

I scrambled through the window and crawled over the bed. Willie T. sat up, and the two of us silently surveyed his room. A quilt and the pillow were on the floor, along with magazines, comic books, toy trucks and two cap pistols, a baseball bat, marbles, an open pocketknife, and about a hundred green plastic army men. On the table beside the bed was an empty medicine bottle and two sticky-looking spoons, and an open bottle of whiskey. It was one of those flat bottles that can sort of fit in a coat pocket, and it was about half full.

"What in the world is that?" I asked.

"Yeah, it's whiskey all right," he admitted, nodding his head. "Mama..." Willie T. coughed weakly, then continued. "Mama's give me so much cough medicine, we run out of it. So she started givin' me Daddy's whiskey, to try to stop me from coughin' myself to death."

"Does it work?" I asked him.

"Better than the cough medicine. But it tastes just as bad. That's where..."

Willie T. started coughing, waving his arms around like he was fighting for air, trying to speak in between coughs.

"...where she is...gone...to get more medicine."

I was suddenly seized by the desire to get Willie T. and me away from there as fast as possible.

"Well, get your clothes on, and hurry up." I grabbed him by the arm and hauled him off the bed. He stood barefooted, wearing just a pair of short pajama pants, shaking his head wearily.

I looked around the room and spied a pair of shorts and a shirt on the floor. I snatched them up and thrust them into Willie T.'s hands. I was becoming hysterical.

"Hurry up! Put your clothes on, quick! We got to go before Aunt Rachel gets back!"

Protesting weakly, and coughing profusely, he managed to get into the wrinkled shorts and shirt. He just pulled the shorts on over his blue-and-white striped pajama pants, which were about two sizes bigger than the shorts.

"I guess we better take this with us," I told him as I screwed the top onto the bottle of whiskey. "Just in case."

Willie T. put on his red high-top P.F. Flyers, and armed with a magic stick, a map, and half a bottle of whiskey, we made our escape out the window.

"We're gonna be in trouble, Lily C.," he managed to huff as we ran full speed down the hill away from his house.

We ran till we got to the woods between my house and Estaleen's. We were both out of breath, and Willie T. sounded like a squeaking door hinge that needed oil. I took the wrinkled map out of my pocket and held it in front of his red sweating face.

"Look," I panted. "I think we can find Junior if we can figure out the map. Mama told me that every treasure map leads to a different treasure. So...somehow, I just know it's got to work that way."

Willie T. squinted against the bright sunlight and inspected the map. I could see his eyes moving slowly back and forth, his eyebrows squinched together in a tight knot, as he stared at the paper as if seeing it for the first time.

"I thought we was s'pose to find gold, or somethin' like that," he protested. He looked me in the eye, gasped a couple of times then fell flat on the ground in a dead faint.

My first thought was that he really was dead. Then my second thought was that he just couldn't be. Some vague plan of using Studebaker's stick to magically revive my cousin passed through my mind, but instead, in my state of panic, I just started whacking him with it as hard as I could. That revived him.

He grabbed hold of me and we grappled for a while, with him wheezing and trying to get the stick away from me, and me trying to get loose from him. Suddenly Willie T. stopped fighting and just held onto me in a death grip, and coughed one last cough right in my face.

Something black and slimy and sticky flew out of his mouth and hit me in the face. It stuck to my cheek, right under my eye.

Screaming hysterically, I wrenched myself out of Willie T.'s grasp and slapped at my face, frantically trying to get the repulsive thing off of me.

"What was that? What was that?" I screamed, as the hideous thing plopped off my face and landed on the dusty ground at my feet. "Is it a bug? Is it a slimy black bug?"

Instantly, the stories about all Great-granddaddy's hundreds of captured bugs popped into my mind, along with the terrifying thought that somehow Willie T. had swallowed and coughed up a nasty black insect. I stumbled backwards, still frantically scrubbing at my cheek.

Willie T. was looking down, calmly scrutinizing the nasty slimy black object.

"It's a p'simmon seed," he said calmly.

"A persimmon seed?" I screamed. "Where in the world did it come from?"

"Gyaah! You know what, Lily C.? The other day, on the Fourth of July, I found that old p'simmon seed layin' on the ground, and I stuck it in my mouth when we was settin' under that p'simmon tree." Pausing, he rubbed his hands around on his throat, craning his neck out like a chicken and twisting his head from side to side. Then he rubbed his belly enthusiastically. "I bet that seed's been stuck in my throat this whole time, and that's what's been makin' me cough. I ain't had the whoopin' cough at all, and if you hadn't whacked me so hard with that magic stick, I'd of been dead for sure. Suffercated."

I wiped tears from my face, trying to believe that it could possibly be a persimmon seed and not some horrible slimy bug that Willie T. coughed up.

"Don't cry, Lily C.," he said, picking up the magic stick and the bottle of whiskey where I had dropped them on the ground. "I thank I'm gonna be okay now."

He held up the magic stick, looking at it from end to end, then gave it a brisk shake close to his ear like he was trying to see if it made any kind of sound. "Hm! It just goes to show you!" he surmised.

Well, after I had collected myself, we looked at the map for a long time, discussing different parts of it and slowly recognizing familiar features.

"Look right there," he announced, jabbing the map with one finger of his right hand while still gingerly massaging his recently afflicted throat with his left hand. "That's Widder Woman Holler, right there."

"Are you sure?" I asked, looking skeptically from the map to my cousin's sweaty face. "How can you tell?"

"I know it is. That's where I went with Mama and Granny Rilla one time, last summer, to pick wild

91

greens, and I was barefooted and I stepped on a briar. And when I set down to get the briar out of my foot, I set down in a ant bed." He nodded his head emphatically and jabbed at the map again, then tapped his finger a couple of times on the designated squiggle. "Yep, that's it all right. I remember how we went down that little way, then we went down that little way," he said, tracing the pencil lines as he spoke. "You remember Granny Rilla told us that a long time ago, when she was a little girl, a widder woman lived there that was afraid of her old goat, 'cause she said he talked to her, plain as anything. The old woman's name was Mattie, and the goat would call her name. 'Maaa-tie. Maaa-tie.' And Granny said if you go there at night-time, you can still hear the old widder woman and her goat, talking to each other in the dark."

Willie T.'s voice trailed off, and he stood as still as a frozen statue, holding the map and looking at me with his eyeballs all big around. I felt a creepy feeling on the back of my head like my hair was standing straight up, and I couldn't keep myself from looking around at the woods and hoping I didn't see anything scary.

"Come on, let's hurry up," Willie T. said, giving the map a little shake. "I bet you that Mama's gonna be back from the store any minute, lookin' for me."

We started off through the woods, neither one of us feeling any braver after that scary story, and we passed right behind the blackened rubble that used to be Estaleen's little house. Willie T. shook his head, then pointed off to his left, down a gully into a thicket of dogwoods and blackberry bushes.

"See," he said. "We have to veer off down this-a-way. It's just like on the map."

We walked for a long time, following the map right through the woods and up a trail leading over a hill. The trees were tall and the shade underneath them was dark and cool. Willie T. stopped every once in a while and cocked his head, like he was listening for something.

"You hear anythang?" he asked, his eyes so wide they looked like they'd pop out of his head. But I didn't hear anything.

We stopped at a shallow, clear branch of water.

"Grind Rock Spring," Willie T. announced, then he splashed his face and cupped his hands full of water and drank.

I washed my hands and face and tasted the water. It tasted clean and good. A red-bird sat on a tree limb right over our heads calling, "Sweet bird, sweet bird, sweet William, William, William." I looked around, thinking about Great-granddaddy W.T. I imagined that I could see him sitting beside this clear, slow-moving stream, scribbling in his journal, wearing an old hat with various weeds and wild flowers stuck all over the floppy brim. Looking down into the clear water, I saw a little craw-dab on the sandy bottom, and when I touched him with my finger he scooted backwards under the edge of a rock.

"I like this place," I said, slowly beginning to remember something I had been told about this very spot.

"Willie T., do you remember Granny Rilla talking about that time when she was a little girl, when she and Great-granddaddy W.T. saw the perfect little woman drowning in the water?

"Yeah..." Willie T. answered slowly. "Yeah, I do."

"Well, this is it. This is where they saw her. I

remember now, Granny said it was at Grind Rock Spring. They were walking along the edge here, and some trash and twigs had washed up against the edge of the water, and they heard something splashing and thought at first that it was a fish splashing around. And they heard a squeaking sound, like a mouse or a chipmunk or a rabbit when it's caught by a cat. When they got over to where it was, they saw it was a little tiny woman in the water right up near the bank, and she was tangled up in the sticks and twigs in the water and she was drowning. Her long hair was all tangled in the trash at the edge of the water and she was trying to swim and get away."

"And she was nekkid," Willie T. added, looking at me with a startled expression on his face.

"That's right. She didn't have on any clothes. Granny said she and Great-granddaddy were both scared and didn't want to mess with her at first, but they could see that she was gonna die if they didn't help her. Granny started crying and said 'Do somethin', do somethin', she's drowning!' And Great-granddaddy knelt down in the edge of the water and got his britches all muddy and wet, and reached into the water and got her untangled from the leaves and twigs, even though he was afraid to touch her. And Granny said she was "a perfect little woman", just about as tall as your hand, and she was making sounds like she was talking to them, but they couldn't understand what she was saying and she looked like she was afraid of them. Granny Rilla was crying and wanted to take her home with them, 'cause she looked like she was nearly dead from drowning, but Great-granddaddy said it wouldn't be right. He said that people would find out and put her in a circus or

94

something. So they put her on a big chip of tree bark and Great-granddaddy W.T. covered her up with his handkerchief 'cause she was cold and shivering, and she floated off down the spring, sittin' on that chip of wood, and . . ."

"Listen," Willie T. whispered, and he held up his hand for me to be quiet. "Do you hear that?"

I stopped talking and listened, but at first I didn't hear a thing. The woods were suddenly very quiet; I didn't even hear any birds or squirrels making any noise. Then, off in the woods somewhere I could hear someone singing. It was quiet for a while, then the singing started up again.

> A poor soul sat sighing by a sycamine tree.
> Sing all a green willow.
> Her hand on her bosom, head on her knee.
> Sing willow, willow, willow.

We looked at each other, listening, but the singing had stopped.

"What in the world was that?" Willie T. asked. I had to declare that I didn't know, and we started through the woods toward the place where the singing had come from. As soon as we started walking, the singing started up again.

> Sing oh the green willow.
> Prithee, hie thee; he'll come anon.
> Sing all a green willow;
> My true love he is a'gone

The voice was so quavery and lonesome sounding, I felt like a possum had run over my grave, and it made the hair on my arms stand up. Coming out through a bunch of thick leafy bushes, we discovered a dusty old driveway curving up to a dilapidated sprawling old house with a wide porch clinging feebly across the front. The mournful singing continued inside the dark house.

"I know this place," I whispered.

Willie T. and I pushed our way out of the bushes and walked slowly up the dusty, weedy path, right up to the porch of the abandoned old house.

"I've been here before. I know who used to live here. This is Aunt Lexie and Uncle Jim's old house."

We stepped up onto the shady front porch where blue and purple morning-glories had taken over the posts and banisters. Three hummingbirds chased each other around the trailing morning-glories; one of them flew straight up to my face and paused, looking right at me like he was telling me hello. I felt like we were in a fairy tale place, everything was so peaceful and beautiful. Inside the house, the singing continued.

I knew that voice.

It was dim inside the house, but a window was open, letting the afternoon light flood in. I could see dust floating magically in the sunlight as it slanted across the room.

"Henry Hope?" I called, my voice echoing through the empty old house. "Is that you?"

A sudden commotion started up in the back of the house; skittering noises as things bumped and fell on the floor, then silence.

Then, a reserved, happy-sounding voice answered back.

"Lily Claire Carlisle...Nash? Is *that* you?"

Willie T. grinned and looked at me, his mouth

falling open in surprise. We stepped into the back room, the old kitchen, still crowded with a huge wooden table and several worse-for-wear chairs. The orange kitten, Shoo-fly, jumped up onto the table, arching his back and meowing to be petted.

Henry Hope stood expectantly beside the table, holding Baby Junior Howard.

Henry Hope and Willie T. and I looked at each other, all three of us flabbergasted, I guess. Baby Junior, resting in the curve of Henry Hope's left arm, kicked his legs and squealed ecstatically. Suddenly Willie T. slapped both his hands with a loud smack against his brown khaki shorts which were ballooning out over his blue-and-white striped pajama pants.

"Henry Hope," he demanded authoritatively, "just what in the world are you doin' way out here with that damn baby?"

Henry Hope gasped, clutching Junior protectively to his thin chest. "Cud'n Lily! Does he talk…that way, all the time?"

I glanced at Willie T., as if examining him to find an answer.

"Yep, he does," I confirmed.

"We nearly kilt ourselves thrashin' through them woods a-lookin' for that baby! And me with the near-about whoopin' cough!" Willie T. exclaimed. "Why are you way out here in the woods with Estaleen's baby?"

"It's a…long…story," Henry Hope stated cordially.

"Oh, me," I sighed, collapsing onto one of the rickety chairs. Willie T. sat down beside me, shaking his head. Then Henry Hope sat down with Junior on his lap. I put the treasure map, Studebaker's magic stick, and the bottle of whiskey on the table. Henry Hope stared at the objects, but didn't say anything.

Baby Junior was wearing one of his tiny white undershirts with snaps across the shoulder, but instead of a diaper there was something that looked suspiciously like a pillow case, white with red roses, tied clumsily around his bottom. Obviously all the baby diapers had burned up in the house fire, so I chose not to ask about the pillowcase.

"What have you been feeding him?" I asked.

Shoo-fly twirled around on the table, knocking over the whiskey bottle. I picked up the bottle, finally feeling a little nervous about having it with us.

"He doesn't like...wild plums. And he...doesn't like soda-crackers. So, he says to me, 'Henry Hope, feed me...buttermilk.' So I just sneaked...over to my house and got some...buttermilk out of my ice-box. He likes...buttermilk."

The baby squealed again, waving his hands and kicking his feet wildly.

"But Estaleen is worried about her little baby. You need to take him back to her," I explained. I glanced over at Willie T. and saw that he had gone to sleep with his head down on the table. His mouth was open and he was breathing softly.

Henry Hope looked at me, his eyes wide with shock.

"That...little mama...is plumb dead! Her house burnt up and I...pulled her out. But she was plumb dead...and that's why I kept this little boy baby."

"No, Henry Hope. She's not dead. She's in the hospital, awful sick, but she's not dead. And the police have got Studebaker in jail, accused of kidnapping Junior. And what about Cowboy? You should have carried the baby to Cowboy."

"Ooooh!" Henry Hope wailed loudly, his big eyes

filling with tears. "I'm...afraid of that ole Cowboy! He likes to jump out...at me and...scare me with his big ole...wolfeener noises! And I said to myself...Henry Hope, that Cowboy would scare this poor little 'un...to death."

I got up and went over to Henry Hope and put my arms around his shoulders, hugging him close to me.

'Oh no, Cowboy is a really good daddy. He loves Baby Junior an awful lot. Now, don't you see, we got to get the baby back to his mama and daddy, somehow?"

Just then, Willie T. woke up and raised his head and announced, "I'm hungry!"

"It's getting late," I told him. "We've got to hurry up and carry Junior back to town and get Henry Hope back to his house..."

"They'll put your crazy cousin in the nut-house for sure, Lily C. You know it?" Willie T. picked up the magic wand and waved it toward Henry Hope's face. "And it won't be nothin' we can do about it, if they find out he's been draggin' that little baby all through these woods with a piller case on its behind and a map on its tongue already."

"That...buttermilk cured that map," Henry Hope mumbled defensively. "And I will not go...to a nut...house."

Willie T. jumped up from his chair, scraping it noisily across the floor, and hopped over to stare at Baby Junior's mouth.

"Is it really?" he chirped. "Is it gone?"

He poked his finger cautiously at the corner of the baby's mouth, and Junior yawned, sticking out a smooth, unmarked tongue.

"Well, would you look at that, Lily C.!" Willie T. exclaimed. "That map's gone off of his tongue, clean as a whistle!"

Henry Hope looked puzzled.

"Ever'body knows that...buttermilk...will cure a map on a baby's...tongue!"

Nine

The Fool-Proof Plan

When Willie T. came up with an idea of how we could straighten everything out, I knew right off that he was on his way to becoming a famous hero, just like the ones Miss Tweedy had told us about. He knew that to keep Henry Hope from being put in the nut-house, and to keep Studebaker Freeman out of the Birmingham jail, we had to get Baby Junior back home to Estaleen and Cowboy without letting anybody know where we'd found him. It really amazed me when he came up with a fool-proof plan.

First of all, he went out onto the front porch of the old house, and wrapped morning-glory vines all around his head. By this time, Henry Hope and I were getting interested in what Willie T. was up to, so we helped him wrap the flowering vines all around himself and the laughing, kicking baby. Of course, Willie T. started fussing and scratching.

"These vines is makin' me itch!" he complained. "If I ain't got the whoopin' cough, I'll die of the nettle rash, sure as the world."

He rubbed dirt all over his face and hands, and then he swallowed two big drinks of the whiskey, shuddering and dancing a jig after each swallow.

"By the time I get home with Baby Junior Howard, I'll be as drunk as Cooter Brown!" he announced. "Won't nobody be able to get the truth out of me." Then he burped so loud the house shook, and he added with a grin, "I won't even know the truth myself!"

The sun was going down toward the west and Henry Hope and I stood on the shadowy front porch watching as my crazy cousin headed east. Henry Hope called out, "South. Head south." And he pointed with his long thin hand toward the woods, the way he wanted Willie T. to go. Willie T. changed directions and tore out through the bushes, waving Studebaker Freeman's magic wand in one hand and carrying Baby Junior piggyback, into the deep woods toward home.

Henry Hope and I went back inside the house and sat down at the old kitchen table, and he told me how on the morning of the fire, he and Studebaker had spent the whole morning all over the place, looking for Shoo-fly. Then, just when they were about to give up, Studebaker found the kitten up a tall sycamore tree, and when he climbed up the tree to rescue the poor little scared thing, he saw smoke.

"And he calls down...to me, 'Henry Hope, it's sure as the world somebody's house...a'burnin' up.' And he leapt...down out of that sycamine tree, and he put a...box...over my Shoo-fly. And we both run...to that Howard house."

Henry Hope ran his fingers through his thin hair, then pointed with his long finger on the wooden table, like he was showing me the burning house, and where he and Studebaker ran up onto the porch and in the front door. He said they heard the baby crying before they got inside, and that the smoke was thick and the two of them got down on their hands and knees, thinking they'd have to crawl all the way through the house. But as soon as they had crawled a little way into the living room, they came across Estaleen laying on the floor, with Baby Junior right beside her kicking and crying!

"And that Studebaker...says to me, 'You get them out from here. I'll have to see...if it's another soul...in this house.' And...I grabbed the baby under one arm, and the mama...under the t'other arm, and...out I went!"

Henry Hope shook his head, looking down at his hands, and told me how he thought he'd never see Studebaker alive again, but in just about a minute, Stu came crawling out onto the front porch and tumbled down the steps, coughing and holding onto Cowboy's ruined old Rickenbacker guitar, burnt to a turn.

"And he put down that burnt-up guitar and...took a look at that woman, and he shook his head...and he says to me, 'Henry Hope, I'm a colored man. I can't have nothin'...to do with no dead...white woman.' So he tells me to take that ...baby to the police."

Henry Hope shivered in the darkening, hot old kitchen. "But I was...skeered . . .Lily Claire. So, I run home to my mama's house...right here...with that boy baby in one arm and my Shoo-fly...in the t'other."

He wiped tears from his face with the back of his thin, bony hand.

"So, there you...have it," he sighed.

We sat in the dark kitchen a little while, without saying anything else. The moon came up, full and round, and the moonlight shone through the open kitchen window. Way far out in the woods I heard old Bu, the hoot owl, and I told Henry Hope I thought we better get home.

We cleaned up all the mess he had made in the house best we could, then he picked up Shoo-fly and I picked up the whiskey bottle and the crumpled map, and we walked out onto the front porch. The night air felt surprisingly cool. When we stepped out into the yard, the moonlight was so bright it looked almost like daytime, except everything looked silvery and still. I imagined Willie T. making his way through the woods in the dark, and a wave of fear came over me.

"Do you think he'll make it through the woods okay?" I asked.

Henry Hope hesitated just a second, then replied, "If he just don't...hit a snag."

We made our way wearily through the woods and it was dark as pitch under the tall trees. Henry Hope held my hand and told me I didn't need to be scared, 'cause he wasn't afraid of the dark. And as we walked through the woods he told me how he and Harold, when they were little boys, would go out at night and sit under a big old oak tree and tell stories in the dark, and listen to the hoot owl in the tree above them. And he said that once Harold had told him, "Henry Hope, I bet you that if we wanted to, we could fly right up there, and sit on that limb, and pay company to that old owl."

"And that's what we done," Henry Hope reported, nodding his head. He looked down at me and squeezed my hand softly. "We flown right up there...and set right on that ...limb. And that ole owl just spied at us...with his big round eyes. And we talked a while. And that's when he told us...his name was...Bu. Then, me and Harold, we flown down...again."

We walked on, quietly, then Henry Hope added, "It was a spell. And me and Harold...felt right strangely for a while. We never told our mama nothin' about it. But then Harold, he told me, 'Henry Hope, that old Bu will...watch out for you if you're ever in the woods...at night.' So...there you have it."

I looked up at Henry Hope, to try to see if he was telling me a tale, but his face looked soft and calm, like he was remembering something serious. He held Shoo-fly up and rubbed his cheek against the kitten's soft fur, and repeated, "There you have it."

After the long walk through the woods, when we finally got to Henry Hope's little house, he was still worried about Junior and what Cowboy might do. We sat down on the front porch steps, and he petted the orange kitten until it went to sleep on his knee.

"I would have never took that...little 'un," he said. "But I thought its mama was plumb dead...and that Studebaker, he said he was a'skeered to touch a white woman...and I got skeered...to go to the law. My brother...Harold, always used to tell me, 'Henry Hope, you got to always remember...to dodge the law.' "

Henry Hope paused, and stopped petting Shoo-fly and just let his arms drop down at his sides.

"Now, you'll have to tell Sam Nash...to get that Studebaker Freeman...out of the jail house. Reckon he didn't...dodge the law...quick enough. But he didn't do nothin' wrong. He didn't do nothin' but help me...find my kitten. And he spied that smoke. And he crawled...all through that burnin'...house. It don't do to study...what would of happened, if he hadn't gone up that...sycamine tree! Now, if he don't get out of the jail house...who will I go fishin'...with?"

I promised him that everything would be okay. But I was tired and anxious and still had a long walk in the dark to get home and see if I could find out what had happened when Willie T. turned up with Baby Junior on his back.

I knew for sure that I was in a good deal of trouble about being gone all day, and for coming home up the mountain in the dark. As it turned out, I was saved by the fact that Mama had stayed at the hospital with Estaleen that night, so I didn't much have to deal with anybody but Daddy. Of course when I came dragging in, tired and dirty with leaves and twigs all in my hair, he was perched out on the front porch steps, his face all worried and looking like he was just about to take off running when he saw me. But he just held onto the porch post and said, "They! I was just about to come looking for you!"

I told him I had been out helping Henry Hope look for Shoo-fly, and he acted like he believed that story.

"So, Henry Hope's back home now, with his kitten?" he asked.

"Yep, he's home with his kitten," I answered wearily.

Daddy hugged me real tight and said, "Well, I guess that was the right thing for you to do, baby." He held me real tight for a long time, patting me on the back of my head and sort of humming, "Umm, um, um." Then he planted a little kiss on top of my head and added, "But I'm mighty glad you're home."

I don't know why I started crying then, but I did, and I hugged my Daddy's neck and sobbed, "I'm glad I'm home, too."

Daddy picked a few twigs out of my hair, there on the dark front porch.

"Your head looks like a stump full of granddaddies," he said.

Then I trailed into the house and barely made it into my room, I was so tired. I lay down on my red calico Drunkard's Path quilt and went to sleep, wondering about Willie T. and Baby Junior.

Ten

Hitting a Snag

As tired as I was, if somebody hadn't woke me up, I would have slept till the cows came home. But I had only been asleep about an hour or two when a noise at my window pulled me out of a deep sleep. I was so worn-out, I heard the noise but couldn't get myself all the way awake, and for a while my mind just whirled around and around, like I was in a deep black ocean, trying to get my head up out of the dark water.

From somewhere out at the edge of the black ocean, I could hear someone whispering my name, and I tried so hard to wake up, it felt like I was trying to lift the heavy dark water up off of me.

Then suddenly I popped up to the surface, like a red and white fishing float, and my eyes opened to the moon-lit dimness of my bedroom.

"Lily Claire? Lily...Claire? You need to wake up here."

The soft whispers were coming from the dark right outside my bedroom window. I sat up and looked face-to-face with Henry Hope.

"Oh, lordy," I sighed, using one of Willie T.'s

Sweet Music on Moonlight Ridge

favorite expressions. "Henry Hope? What is it, now?" I was so bone-tired, it felt like I might die right then and there.

"Lily Claire," he whispered anxiously, so soft it was barely any sound at all. "I couldn't sleep for worryin' about that...Willie T. So, I got out'n bed, and...I walked all around town, just a'lookin'. And, Lily Claire, they ain't no commotion...a'tall."

I rubbed my eyes and ran my fingers through my tangled hair. I pondered over what he was saying, and it came to me that there could be a problem. Henry Hope continued.

"I just laid low in the...bushes, first one place...then t'other. I seen that John Law, Clyde Tucker, drivin' around like a big muckety-muck with his...eyeballs peeled, and a'blowin' that sireen up and down the road. But the whole town is just as quiet, and...I said to myself, 'Henry Hope...that Willie T. hadn't made it out...of the woods with that little 'un a'tall.' Now, we'll have to...go a'lookin' for 'em."

"Go a'lookin'?" I repeated sleepily.

"Yep, sure as I'm a'standin'...here. If'n he had made it back with that...little 'un, why, the whole town would be...millin' and spinnin'. He ain't here...sure as the world."

"Oh, Willie T." I groaned, and tears filled my sleepy eyes.

"Now, it ain't no need to start...bawlin'. We'll have to go back...through them woods and..."

Henry Hope stopped whispering as he watched me buckling my sandals. I had gone to sleep in the same sundress I had worn the day before, so all I had to do was put on my shoes. My legs were all scratched up from trailing through the woods already, and there

109

were still a few twigs and scraps of leaves in my hair.

"And we'll find 'em," Henry Hope finished his sentence. "You got to come...out'n the winder here, so you won't wake up that...Sam Nash."

We looked at each other and listened to the racket coming from the bedroom where Daddy was sleeping. He was snoring so loud, I figured if the noise he was making didn't wake him up, nothing would.

We slipped noiselessly across the yard and plunged back into the woods, pretty much following the same trail Willie T. and I had traveled the day before. Moonlight almost as bright as daylight lit our way, but there were a few dark clouds that passed over the moon from time to time. Once we were deep into the woods, it got harder and harder to see where we were going.

"How will we ever figure out where to look?" I asked, grasping Henry Hope's hand in the dark.

Henry Hope answered that he had pointed Willie T. toward the south, and if he had stayed true, we should cross his path in the direction we were headed.

"He's some'ers in these woods; we'll come across't him. Drunk, I s'pect, and...asleep under a tree."

Then with no warning at all, "Willie T. Nock!" my normally soft-spoken cousin bellowed beside me. I like to jumped out of my skin.

"He'll hear us a'comin," Henry Hope assured me. So, we both started calling out Willie T.'s name as we struggled through the dark woods.

We listened for a reply, but heard nothing.

Suddenly, a terrible noise of flapping and whooping descended on us, and Bu, the hoot-owl, almost hit us in the face, scaring me and Henry Hope nearly to death. We stopped dead in our tracks, clutching ahold of each other until we had regained ourselves a little.

Bu, meanwhile, came back toward us, barely missing the top of Henry Hope's head, then sailed soundlessly away ahead of us.

"There you have it! That Bu is a'showin' us the way," Henry Hope announced.

We followed the big old owl the best we could, sometimes losing him in the trees. He'd come sailing back toward us, and hover right in front of our faces, then off he'd fly again, into the dense woods. Meanwhile, clouds were gathering, getting thicker and thicker, and I smelled rain.

"Willie T. Nock!" we both yelled every once in a while. "Willie T. Nock!"

Bu disappeared entirely, and we stopped walking, just straining our ears to see if we could hear anything in the dark. I was getting scared, and pressed myself as close to Henry Hope as I could get.

"You reckon we've come the right way?" I asked, my voice shaky and weak.

Henry Hope reared back with his head thrown back, fists clenched and arms straight and stiff down by his sides.

"Willie T." he hollered like a crazy person. "Willie T. Nock!"

The woods around us grew still and silent, and far out in front of us, a voice called out, barely loud enough for us to hear.

"Ah minna hoe..."

Henry Hope and I looked at each other for just a second, then we both tore out through the thicket in the direction of the strange and distant sound. We stopped, and this time we heard someone singing softly. No doubt about it; it was "Au Clair de la Lune."

"Willie T.!" I squealed, as Henry Hope stopped and bellowed again in his new loud voice.

Out ahead of us, the singing stopped, and the voice called once again, "Ah minna hoe!" Then the sweet singing resumed.

Henry Hope and I were running full speed when we came to a clearing, just as a loud clap of thunder broke above us, and a few raindrops began falling noisily onto the pinestraw and dry leaves around us.

"Willie T.? Where are you at?" I called.

"Watch out!" Willie T.'s unmistakable voice answered us. "Ah'm in a *hole!*"

We continued to run blindly toward the sound of his voice, unable to see anything as storm clouds totally covered the moon and more drops of rain fell around us.

Just then, Bu swooped down in front of us, and Henry Hope and I stumbled into each other and came to a standstill. "It's a HOLE!" Willie T's voice warned us loudly, coming from somewhere down below us. "I'm down here!"

Henry Hope and I finally understood what we were hearing, and we slowly stooped down to the ground, discovering that, sure enough, we were both right on the edge of a large round hole in the ground. If we had taken one more step, that's where we would have wound up.

"Lord save us tonight!" Henry Hope exclaimed. "He's in a...hole!"

"Yep, I damn sure am!" an exasperated voice replied.

Henry Hope and I leaned our heads over the edge of the hole, trying to catch a glimpse of Willie T.

"You got that little 'un? Are ye okay down there?" Henry Hope called.

"Junior's fine, I'm fine," Willie T. answered irritably from out of the dark hole. "It woulda probably killed me, fallin' in here, but I landed on my springy legs. Mostly I just been waitin' and dodgin' dead mice."

"Dead mice?" Henry Hope and I both repeated at the same time.

"Yes, lordy!" Willie T.'s strident voice replied. "That crazy old owl has throwed dead mice down here on me, the whole time I been down here!"

Henry Hope had started moving around and reaching down into the dark hole. A cloud moved out from in front of the moon, and for just a few seconds, we could see all around us. I watched Henry Hope sit back on his haunches, then quickly survey the hole and the clearing around us.

"I'll be John...Brown. This here's the old church well. You done fell in the old... church well!" he hollered down into the hole.

"You wanta get me out?" Willie T. asked.

Henry Hope lay flat on his belly and dangled his arm into the hole, just as the clouds covered the moon and everything went totally black. The wind picked up and began to howl through the trees, and a storm broke for real.

"Grab aholt," he instructed, over the noise of the increasing storm. "You best grab...a few of them...dead mice. He's been a'tryin' to...feed you."

Henry Hope continued moving and reaching down into the hole. "It would not be polite...to refuse a good dead mouse...from a' owl."

"Gyaah!" was the only answer from the hole. Then Henry Hope grunted and pulled his arm up out of the dark well, and there was my Willie T., hanging on for dear life with one hand, and the other arm wrapped around a sleeping baby.

By this time, a violent storm was right on top of us. The rain was pouring down, thunder and lightning were crashing, and tree limbs had started breaking and hitting the ground around us. Henry Hope gathered me and Willie T. and Baby Junior in his long arms, and we all gazed around in a panic, tryin' to decide which way to run.

Across the clearing, I could barely make out the shape of an old wooden structure. By the eerie glow of a flash of lightning, I saw that it was an old wooden church.

"Look, Henry Hope!" I tugged at his wet sleeve, then pointed through the rain toward the dark building. "Let's go there!"

For some reason, Henry Hope hesitated, and he made a funny little sound and held us a little tighter, bending over to try to protect us from the wind and rain.

"Come on!" Willie T. yelled. "If I ain't killed a'fallin' in that hole, I'll be drownded in this storm!"

"Well...let's see," Henry Hope muttered, and the three of us dashed for the old church house.

Once we were inside, the storm seemed to get even worse outside.

"Hit's a cyclone...sure as the world," Henry Hope stated ominously.

The church house was bare of any furniture, several windows were broken out, and the wooden floor was littered with scattered leaves and limbs and dirt. We heard a whooshing sound, and big old Bu came in through a broken window, perched on the rain-drenched windowsill, and ruffled his feathers with a loud shake.

Then, following Henry Hope's orders, the three of us made a big show of making like we were eating the dead mice that Willie T. had crammed in his pockets. Bu stared at us with his huge round eyes, then calmly went to grooming his feathers.

Baby Junior had been awake for a while, and Willie T. dangled a dead mouse in front of his face, waving it back and forth and chanting, "Lookee, lookee. It's a dee-licious mouse!"

Junior watched the mouse swinging back and forth, then began kicking his feet wildly, and waved one fist toward the small damp rodent.

The storm began to calm down, just as sudden as it had started, and off in the woods came the unmistakable wail of the wolfeener. We all froze.

I looked up at Henry Hope, and saw that his eyes were big and round and he peered around first one way then another, like he was seeing which way to run. Seconds later, the dreadful howl broke the silence again, this time a whole lot closer to us than it had been the first time.

"What is that?" I asked, even though I knew for sure what it was.

"It's that booger," Henry Hope replied in a low, scary voice.

"Is it gonna get us?" I whispered, barely able to make a sound.

Henry Hope looked around us again, then answered calmly, "No. Hit can't smell us... in here. Hit will pass right by."

We cringed as we heard one more blood chilling wail out in the dark, and this time it sounded like it was right outside the wall of the church.

Bu, still sitting on the windowsill, opened his huge wings and silently flew away into the night.

Baby Junior flinched at the flapping sound of the big owl's wings.

"Why is he flying away?" I cried.

After a pause, Willie T. looked at the window with an expression of surprise on his wet, dirt-streaked face.

"He's leadin' it away from us," he whispered. "It'll follow him, and he'll lead it off from us."

We sat still for a minute or two, as quiet as the dead mice in our hands. The storm had passed as fast as it had started, and we all began to relax and yawn. Willie T. rocked the baby back and forth, and soon Junior was sound asleep again.

Without saying a word, we all got up off the dusty floor, and crept out into the still, wet darkness. Henry Hope cocked his head to listen, didn't hear anything, then led us across the old empty churchyard and back into the woods, headed for Eden.

Henry Hope was determined to escort Willie T. as close as possible to the edge of town, and the further we walked, the drier everything got. By the time we reached the outskirts of Eden, it looked like it hadn't been raining there at all.

"Now, I'm tellin' you young'uns, and you pay...attention," Henry Hope announced before letting Willie T. continue into town by himself. "We're not to tell a soul...about us takin' cover in that ol'...church house."

I was too tired to argue, but I wondered why in the world he'd say any such a thing to us. The look on

Willie T.'s face told me that he suspected that something was up, but he just shrugged, hitched Baby Junior up on his hip, and started off down the road. After a few steps, he turned around and came back.

"Here, you take this," he told me, and handed me Studebaker's magic stick. "I thought for sure I'd have to fight that wolfeener off with it. But, now you better keep it."

Then, off he went, humming in the dark like everything was just fine.

Henry Hope sighed and rubbed his hand across his forehead.

"I'm a'takin' you home, Lily Claire Nash," he sighed. "Then I'm a'goin' home…to bed. My Shoo-fly must be thinkin'…I'm plumb lost and gone."

Eleven

Home at Last

So, that's how Willie T. Nock got to be a hero. The way the story goes, he barely made it out of the woods and was meandering down main street with Baby Junior, when he was spotted by Police Chief Clyde Tucker. Willie T., everybody knew, had the whooping cough and had wandered away from home, delirious with a fever, and they say he was reeking with the whiskey and cough medicine that Aunt Rachel had been giving him. And they say he was talking out of his head about following a big possum into the woods and finding Junior sleeping in a hollow tree with a bunch of baby possums. The editor of the Eden Daily News was right there, Johnny-On-the-Spot, and he took a picture of Willie T. all wrapped in morning-glory vines and covered with dirt, holding the sleeping baby. Then they whisked Willie T. and the baby to the hospital and finally got Baby Junior reunited with his mama and daddy.

Mama was there when Aunt Rachel and Uncle Buddy arrived at the hospital to pick up Willie T., and she says that Estaleen and Cowboy were beaming and crying with joy, they were so happy to get their little baby back. Estaleen hugged Willie T., and hugged him and hugged him, and would have kissed him a big one if Willie T. would've let her. They say Cowboy was all choked up and could barely talk when he said, "Young feller, you got my eternal thanks. You've saved us, total."

"I'll swun, it's the Gospel truth," Estaleen told Police Chief Clyde Tucker. "That boy has sure saved our Junior's life. Whoo-eee!"

The next day the picture of Willie T. and Baby Junior was on the front page of the Sunday newspaper, and the big headline said,

Howard Infant Stolen by Large Opossum, Rescued by Boy Hero

Early Sunday morning, Brother Goforth got a big delegation together and we all went to the jailhouse to make sure Studebaker was turned loose without any trouble. Oley Hutchins and a few of his buddies were milling around outside the jail, but they weren't dressed up in their sheets. When they saw Brother Goforth cutting his eyes around at them, they all scattered like chickens in a hail storm.

Clyde Tucker had to wake Stu up to let him out of jail, and Stu was mad as the Dickens, with his old lips poked out. He straightened out his clothes, rubbed his eyes and told Police Chief Tucker that he ought to be ashamed for locking up innocent people with absolutely no incriminatory evidence whatsoever and not so much as a writ of habeas corpus, and that he was sure enough lucky that Stu's famous lawyer brother from New Orleans hadn't arrived yet to straighten things out.

"You know, Chief Tucker," Studebaker added, drawing himself up tall and straight, "you have an extremely parsimonious attitude, and a piss-poor jail to boot!"

"Now, Studebaker. That ain't no way for you to talk. I want you to quit talkin' attaway," Clyde warned, trying to look threatening.

Studebaker Freeman never missed a beat. "Clyde Tucker, you might want horns, but you'll die butt-headed!" he pronounced, leveling his gaze right at the police chief's red face.

Clyde turned his hands palm up in front of him, like he had nothing to hide.

"Yeah, I reckon you're right about that. That's what my mama always told me!" he answered, and we all had a good laugh.

All the stores were closed on Sunday, but Police Chief Tucker, I guess trying not to be too parsimonious and butt-headed, made them open up the Jitney Jungle grocery store to get Stu some new cardboard boxes and paper sacks. When I returned his magic stick to him, Studebaker lowered his eyebrows and stared at me for a few seconds. Then he shook the stick real hard a few times, looked it up and down, then shook it again.

"Um-hmm," he grunted. "You don't need to be messin' with this! You young childrens sure could have done some meanness with this thing. I believe I got it back just in time. Um-hmm, just in time."

Because the Howards didn't have a house anymore, Uncle Junebug Isbell donated some lumber from his sawmill where Cowboy worked, and Daddy and Henry Hope and Cowboy fixed up Aunt Lexie and

Uncle Jim's old house for Cowboy and Estaleen and Junior to live in. When they were finished, it looked just like a story-book house, and Estaleen kept the morning-glory vines all over the front porch.

"I'll swun, it's shore enough the prettiest house on Moonlight Ridge," she told me. "Whoo-ee!"

Uncle Buddy Nock gave Cowboy an old beat-up guitar that he'd had forever and never learned to play. For the rest of that summer, we'd all gather of an evening on the big front porch of Estaleen and Cowboy's beautiful house to listen to Cowboy playing the guitar and Estaleen singing all the strange, haunting songs she knew, with Studebaker sitting on the porch steps, waving his magic wand like an orchestra conductor.

Mama and Estaleen always made a pallet of soft quilts for Baby Junior and Willie T. and me, and we'd lie on the cool soft quilts, watching millions of lightning bugs, *Lampyridae coleoptera*, in the black night and listening to the sweet music, and whispering about first one thing and another.

One night out on Estaleen's porch, I asked Willie T. if he had any idea why Henry Hope had warned us not to ever mention seeing the old church out in the woods. Willie T. looked at me straight in the eye and said that he'd told Aunt Rachel about seeing the old church on his way back home after rescuing Baby Junior away from the angry mama possum. Aunt Rachel told him there was no church out there anymore, and hadn't been for years. There had been one there a long time ago, she said, but it had got deserted and dilapidated, and it fell down way back when she and Mama were little girls. She told him it was just his imagination from being delirious with the

121

whooping cough.

That sure gave me a spooky feeling, and we went back to listening to the music and listening to the grown-ups laugh and talk, and I never said a word about it again.

After a while, Henry Hope got so that he'd sidle up to Cowboy when he was playing the guitar, watching every move and leaning down so close it looked like he was gonna stick his nose in the strings. So Cowboy started showing Henry Hope how to play a few songs, and pretty soon Henry Hope turned out to be a really good guitar player. Then Granny Rilla came home from up north in Tullahoma, and just like that, she gave Paw Paw Jack's fiddle to Henry Hope.

"This here's what you need," she told him. And she patted the fiddle as Henry Hope turned it first one way then another. "I always knew you'd make a fiddle player."

Henry Hope and Granny Rilla smiled at each other.

"I ... knowed it, my own self," he told her. Then he touched that bow to the fiddle and made the prettiest sound you ever heard. I reckon he's had that music inside him all the time, and it was just waitin' for the right time to get out.

All the rest of that summer, people all over Eden and out on the mountain talked about how amazing it was, how Willie T. went out in his delirious condition and found the lost baby. Much to my surprise, Willie T. actually never cared to talk about it much, and he never did any bragging about being in the newspaper. He just said it was dark and scary, going through the woods by himself with the sleeping baby on his back, and the whole time he was afraid the wolfeener would get him, or he'd hear the widder woman's goat talking to him, and big old Bu kept swooping down too close to him, scaring him to death. Then, when he fell in the hole, he thought for sure he was a goner, and he figured he'd never make it back home with Baby Junior. He told me that he couldn't remember much of anything else about that whole day and night, because of all the coughing and his empty stomach and the Wild Turkey whiskey and the itching with the nettle rash. But he remembered the old church and the dead mice.

Aunt Rachel got the big-head about her boy being a hero, and she tried to keep him in the house because of his fragile lungs now that he'd had the whooping cough and all. But Uncle Buddy Nock insisted that Willie T. had to keep on playing baseball, so he could grow up to be even more famous than he already was.

And me? That was the summer I learned what it means to be a real hero, and that we ought to treasure every single person because when there's not any ordinary heroes around, just anybody can jump up and be one.

I really do believe Willie T. is a hero, because he went through the scary dark woods by himself and, even after all the trouble he had, he got Baby Junior back home safe, and he got Studebaker Freeman out of jail and he never let on about Henry Hope. I kept that picture from the newspaper of Willie T. wrapped in vines and dirt, and I've still got it stuck on my wall beside Great-granddaddy W.T.'s bug photographs.

But I know for sure that Henry Hope and Studebaker are real heroes too, 'cause they risked their own lives and saved Estaleen and Baby Junior out of that burning house. And Henry Hope kept Baby Junior safe and cured the map on his tongue with buttermilk.

Sometimes, I think about how it was all tied together; how if Henry Hope hadn't had that kitten, and if the kitten hadn't got lost, he and Studebaker wouldn't have ever seen the smoke and wouldn't have discovered Estaleen and Baby Junior in the burning house. And if I hadn't had Studebaker Freeman's magic stick, Willie T. might have died of suffocation with the persimmon seed stuck in his throat.

And crazy old Willie T.? He swears to me that Baby Junior is a hero, too!

"That dang baby found his own self!" he whispers to me, shifting his eyes around to make sure nobody hears him. "If Junior hadn't of had that map on his tongue in the first place, *we* woulda' never found him, sure as the world!"

I don't know why, but it seems like our part of the country just breeds heroes.

I guess it just goes to show you.

Glossary

Arby-vida – arborvitae: an evergreen tree or shrub in the cypress family. In human anatomy, arbor vitae refers to white matter of the cerebellum or a part of the canal of the cervix.

Acadian – French settler who colonized Acadia (Nova Scotia) after 1604; thousands died during the expulsion of Acadians beginning in 1755; many settled in Louisiana.

Boocoos – Southern interpretation of the French beaucoup; lots and lots of anything.

Bu – Apache word for owl.

Craw-dab – childhood term for crawdad, crawfish, crayfish.

Devonette – an upholstered couch or sofa.

French Huguenots – French Protestants, forced by religious persecution to flee France in the 1600s.

Gene Krupa – popular American jazz drummer in 1930s, 40s and 50s.

Map on the tongue – or "geographic tongue"; smooth bright red spots or patches causing the tongue to look like a map. Patches can change size or location from day to day; may   be sore or burn. May be caused by stress or allergies.

Milk teeth – baby teeth

Naiche – Chiricahua Apache name; the second son of Cochise and friend of Geronimo. Chiricahua Apaches lived in Alabama in late 1800s before being sent to Oklahoma.

Pirogue – small flat-bottomed wooden boat, moved through swampy water by pushing with a long pole.

Plymouth Rock wool – pattern or design resembling a black and white barred Plymouth Rock chicken.

Quakers – Christian denomination called The Society of Friends, who came to America in the 1600s hoping to escape religious persecution in England, and who based their beliefs on "Inner Light," or the ability of every person to directly perceive the glory and love of God.

Trillium – a genus of herbs in the lily-of-the-valley family, bearing a whorl of three leaves and a large solitary flower.

Wolfeener – a rarely seen varmint residing in the woods of Alabama.

RECIPES

Granny's Persimmon Cookies

2 tablespoons butter, softened
¼ teaspoon ground nutmeg
1 cup sugar
1 cup persimmon pulp, pureed
1 ½ cups all purpose flour
1 cup chopped walnuts or pecans
1 ½ teaspoons baking powder
½ cup raisins
2 teaspoons baking soda
½ cup chopped dates
1 teaspoon ground cinnamon
1 ½ teaspoons grated orange rind
¼ teaspoon ground cloves
1 teaspoon vanilla extract
¼ teaspoon ground allspice

Heat oven to 375 degrees.

Cream butter in a large mixing bowl; gradually add sugar a little at a time, beating well.

Combine flour, baking powder, soda, cinnamon, cloves, allspice and nutmeg in a small bowl. Add to creamed butter and sugar mixture alternately with pureed persimmons, beginning and ending with flour mixture. Beat well after each addition.
Stir in remaining ingredients.

Drop dough by heaping teaspoons full, 2 inches apart onto lightly greased cookie sheets. Bake at 375 for 8 minutes or until lightly brown. Remove from cookie sheets and cool on wire racks. Yield: about 4 – 5 dozen.

Pecan Pralines

¾ cup white granulated sugar
¾ cup light brown sugar
pinch of salt
½ cup evaporated milk
1 teaspoon vanilla extract
¼ stick butter
1 cup pecan halves

Mix white sugar, light brown sugar and evaporated milk in a medium sauce pan over medium-high heat. Reduce heat to medium-low, cook and stir for about 6 minutes.

When syrup reaches the soft ball stage, remove from heat and add vanilla, salt and butter.
Stir until butter is melted, then add pecan halves.

Beat the candy while it is hot. As soon as it begins to lose its glossy sheen, drop by spoonfuls onto waxed paper placed on a cookie sheet or newspaper.

Makes 12 pralines.

Rilla's Chicken Country Captain

1 frying chicken, cut into pieces
¼ cup flour
1 teaspoon salt
¼ teaspoon black pepper
1 medium diced onion
½ cup diced green bell pepper
2 cloves garlic, crushed
1 tablespoon curry powder
½ teaspoon dried thyme
1 16 oz. can stewed tomatoes
3 tablespoons golden raisins
Vegetable oil/butter mixture for frying

Rinse chicken and pat dry. Dredge chicken pieces in flour, salt, pepper mixture. Heat oil/butter mixture in large skillet. Brown chicken on all sides. Remove chicken and add onion, bell pepper, garlic, curry powder, thyme, and tomatoes to a small amount of oil in skillet. Stir over low heat to mix ingredients.

Return chicken to skillet, add raisins, cover, and cook till tender, about 30 minutes.

Serve over cooked rice.

Serves 4 – 6

Cabbage Chow-Chow

1 small head cabbage chopped
3 cups okra chopped
1 or 2 hot banana peppers chopped
1 green tomato chopped
1 large onion chopped
½ teaspoon salt (or to taste)
¼ teaspoon black pepper
Cooking oil for frying

Heat small amount of cooking oil in heavy skillet. Add all chopped ingredients. Add salt and black pepper. Cook over medium to medium-high heat, stirring frequently, until cabbage and onions appear translucent.

Serve hot with black-eyed peas and cornbread.

Sam Nash's "Secret" Barbecue Sauce

3 cups ketchup
¼ cup brown sugar
½ cup molasses
1 teaspoon vinegar
1 teaspoon prepared mustard
1 cup Worcestershire sauce
½ teaspoon garlic powder

Combine all ingredients in a saucepan. Cook over low heat while preparing ribs for cooking.

Brush ribs with sauce frequently while cooking close to hot coals on barbecue grill.

Sweet Potato Pie

2 cups mashed cooked sweet potatoes
½ cup honey
½ teaspoon salt
2 eggs
1 cup sugar
1 teaspoon vanilla extract
1 cup pecans chopped

Heat oven to 350.

Mix mashed sweet potatoes, honey and salt.

Beat eggs. Add sugar, vanilla extract, and pecans. Add to sweet potato mixture.

Pour into unbaked pie shell.
Bake at 350 for 1 hour.

Book Club Discussion
Sweet Music on Moonlight Ridge

- What significance or symbolism is suggested by the name of the town, Eden?

- Character flaws often influence a story more than a character's positive attributes do. Did any of the characters have flaws that contributed to the story?

- Do you think children of this era and environment were really free to do the things Lily Claire and Willie T. did?

- In what ways does W.T. Greenberry influence the development of Lily Claire's character and her view of the world around her?

- How do Lily Claire and her family view Studebaker Freeman? What is the Eden community's view of Studebaker?

- In what ways does Studebaker influence the plot, action, and outcome of Sweet Music on Moonlight Ridge?

- How did Studebaker's grandfather influence Studebaker's life and status in the community?

- What information presented early in the story indicates why Studebaker may have been unwilling to examine the unconscious Estaleen to determine her condition? Was Studebaker's declaration "I'm a colored man," the only reason he may have been afraid?

- What traits, abilities, and characteristics made Willie T. able to successfully carry out the rescue of Baby Junior?

- How do the stories that Miss Althea Bibb Tweedy tells her class foreshadow the outcome of Willie T.'s rescue of Baby Junior?

- Are the strange occurrences on Moonlight Ridge due to supernatural manifestations, or manifestations of the characters' imaginations? How does Henry Hope relate to these unusual events?

- What transformations are evident in Henry Hope's character as the story progresses? How do you think Harold's influence affected Henry Hope's development?

- In what scenes does music play an important role?

Ramey Channell

Lily Claire

Possum Pi

Willie T.

Ramey Channell

About the Author

Ramey Channell has had poetry, short stories, and children's stories published by Alabama Writer's Conclave, Scholastic Press, Alabama State Poetry Society, River's Edge Publishing, *Aura Literary Arts Review, Birmingham Arts Journal*, and others. This is her first novel.

She lives in Alabama with her two daughters, one grandson, one dog, seven cats, and countless undomesticated possums.

Ramey is currently working on book two of *The Moonlight Ridge Series,* a short story collection, and an illustrated children's book.

Ramey Channell

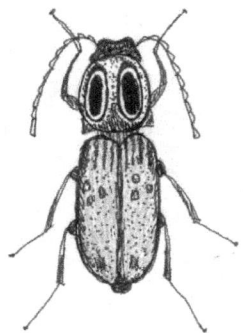

Eyed click beetle, *Alaus oculatus elateridae*

Cicada, *Magicada hemiptera*

Doodle bug, *Hesperoleon abdominalis*

Lightning bug, *Lampyridae coleoptera*

www.ingramcontent.com/pod-product-compliance
Lightning Source LLC
Chambersburg PA
CBHW071959170626
46813CB00005B/1929